Thirteen

For Gill

J.M.

ORCHARD BOOKS
96 Leonard Street, London EC2A 4XD
Orchard Books Australia
32/45-51 Huntley Street, Alexandria, NSW 2015
ISBN 1 84362 492 3 (hardback)
ISBN 1 84362 835 X (paperback)
First published in Great Britain in 2005
First paperback publication in 2005
This collection © John McLay, 2005
The Seal's Fate © Eoin Colfer, 2005
It Must Be her Age © Mary Hooper, 2005
Dumb Chocolate Eyes © Kevin Brooks, 2005
Double Thirteen © Eleanor Updale, 2005
What I Did in my Holidays © Paul Bailey, 2005
Hey! This is Me! © Jean Ure, 2005
bad language © Marcus Sedgwick, 2005
Road Trip © Kay Woodward, 2005
The Wrong Party © Helen Oyeyemi, 2005
The Anorak's First Kiss © John McLay, 2005
On Fire for Thirteen © Margaret Mahy, 2005
You Is a Man Now, Boy © Bali Rai, 2005
Space-Alien Mothers and the Non-Wild, Wild Child © Karen McCombie, 2005
The rights of these authors to be identified as the authors of
these works have been asserted by them in accordance with
the Copyright, Designs and Patents Act, 1988.
A CIP catalogue record for this book is available from the British Library.
3 5 7 9 10 8 6 4 2 (hardback)
1 3 5 7 9 10 8 6 4 2 (paperback)
Printed in Great Britain
www.wattspub.co.uk

Thirteen

Thirteen original stories.
Thirteen outstanding authors.

Edited by

John McLay

ORCHARD BOOKS

Contents

1

The Seal's Fate

by Eoin Colfer

The Seal's Fate

The baby seal looked at Bobby Parrish through round black eyes. Cute if you liked that sort of thing. If you were a girl with posters of sad-eyed French kids all over your room. Boys didn't do cute. Boys caught fish and gutted them and fed their innards to the gulls. Boys killed things because that was how life was, and you'd better be ready for it when school was over. Bobby knew that when Saint Brendan's doors closed behind him for the last time, he would strip off his uniform put on some oilskins and take his berth on *The Lady Irene.*

Still, the seal was cute. Bobby could admit that much to himself, as long as no one was around. He was careful to think it quietly, in case one of his friends was telepathic. The animal's black nose quivered and white sunspots spread across its back like a mane. Cute. But like Dad said, it was vermin.

Bobby crawled a couple of feet closer, careful not to startle the seal. Limestone crags pressed into his stomach, and rock-pool slime destroyed his jeans. It didn't matter. A working man had to be able to ignore discomfort to get the job done.

The seal watched him calmly. It was not afraid.

9

Quite the opposite, it was pleased at the prospect of company. It arched its back, slapping its flippers on the slick rock. Bobby slapped the rocks himself, trying to get a bit of a rapport going. It seemed to do the trick. The seal stretched its tiny head forward, coughing three short barks.

We're friends now, thought Bobby. Buddies. This seal probably thinks we're going to spend the summer swimming around the bay, fighting crime.

Well, old buddy, sorry to disappoint you, but your future is not going to be quite so rosy.

Bobby reached behind him, wrapping his fingers around the club's taped handle.

Dick Parrish had spoken from *The Lady Irene*'s deck. The young people gathered around the quay walls above, hanging on his every word. The men never spoke to the boys down the dock. This must be important.

Bobby thought his dad was like a different person, surrounded by sea and stone. He was invincible, with wind lines burned into his face, and hands that could strangle a conger eel. Every step he took away from the sea diminished him, until at home he would collapse into the armchair and have someone bring him tea.

But here, he was in his element, and everything about him was fierce.

'It's the seals, boys. They're a bloody plague.'

He called them boys, even though Babe Meara was in the group. Babe considered herself a boy, and anybody who suggested otherwise better have shin guards.

'I saw three today,' cried Seanie Ahern. 'Off the point.'

'There were four!' corrected Seán Ahern, his twin. 'And they were in the bay!'

The Ahern twins would argue about the colour of mud. Their real names were Jesse and Randolph, but who would be mean enough to call them that. Only a parent who loved Westerns.

Dick raised his hands for silence. The brown palms were crisscrossed with white rope burns and welts. Fishing, statistically the most dangerous profession in the world. Two of Dick's brothers hadn't been lucky enough to get off with just rope burns.

'They're everywhere,' he said. 'The bay, the point, even poking their noses into the dock, the cheeky buggers. They're infesting the entire peninsula this year. A fellow I know from Ross reckons the seals are thriving on all the effluent pumped from the factories.'

The Ahern twins giggled and elbowed each other when they realised what that actually meant.

'I wouldn't mind that, if they'd stick to eating waste, but those seals are eating our catch too, and they're ripping the nets apart.'

Everybody knew what that meant. Holes in the nets led to long evenings weaving them back together, with sharp twine wearing grooves in your hands.

'Things are bad enough already this year, without having to put up with these vermin too. We haven't had a sniff of a mackerel all summer and the crabs are either getting smart or scarce.'

The other men nodded, muttering their agreement around roll-up cigarettes. Hard times were upon them, no doubt about it. Duncade was just about fished out, what with the factory trawlers and the Spanish boats sneaking into Irish waters. Mackerel had always been the life's blood of the south east, now there were barely enough fish to bait the pots. There hadn't been a silver sea in years, a time when huge shoals of sprats, the mackerel's meal of choice, swam along the coast and often into the dock itself. When that happened every man, woman and child was pressed into service, and every container from bucket to laundry basket was lowered into the sea to trap the silver-blue fish following the sprats hungrily.

'So, here's the way it's going to be,' said Dick Parrish. 'We're going to fight back. From this day on, there is a bounty on seals.'

Bobby felt a jolt of electricity hop from kid to kid. A bounty meant money, and there is no better way to excite youngsters than with the promise of money.

'Anyone who brings in a seal's flipper gets a crisp pound note from me.'

A pound, thought Bobby. That's an entire day's farm wages. Then he thought of something else.

'A seal's flipper?' he said. 'But that means you would have to...'

'Kill it, son,' said his father flatly. 'Kill it dead with rocks or clubs. I don't care. They are big rats and we will send them packing!'

The others were with Dick, the combination of bloodlust and riches, sending their hearts racing. Seal bounty had been commonplace fifty years ago. All their parents and grandparents had hunted the rocks for extra money. But there hadn't been a bounty in decades. It was most likely illegal.

'I want you to find those rats wherever they try to sun themselves. This summer you will be waiting whenever they poke their shiny heads above the waves. Waiting with something blunt to smite them.

Do you hear me?'

The boys nodded, trying to appear casual before the fishermen. Real men of the sea did not get excited. Moby Dick could breach off their bow, and a real fisherman would spit over the gunwales and pretend not to notice.

'We all know the spots where the seals go. Lure them in with a slab of cod, then let them have it with the club. Take care mind, a bull seal will take a chunk out of your leg with its teeth. Worse still, it will break your bones with a swipe of its tail.'

Bobby felt his heart expand in his chest. He hoped its thumping would not shake his jacket. But he was not ready for all this talk of killing and broken bones. It was too soon. Thirteen years of age. Too young to smoke, but old enough to kill a seal. Bobby glanced around at his companions, Paudie, the twins and Babe Meara. Their eyes were alight. He tried to match their giddiness, for his father's sake.

His father, standing there in command of the whole dock. Bobby realised that Dick Parrish was a leader to all these men. They looked to him for example. It was a crippling year, and damned if Dick hadn't come up with a solution. His father felt the look and threw Bobby a wink.

Be the first, that wink said. Be the first on the slip with a seal's flipper.

Bobby winked back, adding in a grin, but it felt like a sticker, pasted over his real feelings. He didn't want to kill a seal. He didn't know if he could.

The seal's eyes were hypnotic, round, deep and black as though they knew things that you never could. What have you seen? wondered Bobby. Deep ocean chasms? Mysterious tentacled creatures that could swallow a ship? Your family's blood spread across the flat rocks, diluted with every lap of the tide?

'Stop it,' he hissed at the cub. 'I know what you're doing. Trying to make yourself real to me. But it won't work, you're vermin. Nothing more. That's what Dad says, and who am I going to believe? You, a seal I never met before, or my own father?'

Bobby hefted the club. It was a family heirloom. Bobby's grandfather had used it for general clubbing duties in the second half of the last century. Grandad had presented the macabre relic to Bobby when he heard about the bounty.

'I whittled this myself out of a lump of ebony that came off an African wreck. It might be old but, by Jesus, you whack anything living with this and that's all she wrote. See this here...'

Grandad pointed with a nicotine-browned finger to a splat patch on the club. 'That's from a shark that got caught up in the nets one time. I took one eye out of him and half his brain with a single belt. He survived though.' Grandad had lost himself in the memory, gazing out to sea. Looking at things only he could see. 'He's out there now. Half-blind and completely mental. Waiting for me to put so much as a toe in the water.' He handed Bobby the club. 'It's all yours now, boy. Pull well back and follow through. Oh, and wear old clothes. When a seal's bowels go, they go everywhere.'

Bobby ran his finger along the club's grip now. A single strip of hide twisted six inches up the shaft. Grandad claimed to have stripped it from a rhinoceros who ran into his jeep when he was on safari, knocking himself unconscious. The rhinoceros was alive in Africa still, just waiting for Grandad to put so much as a toe inside Kenya... The strap felt like linoleum to Bobby.

The boy stood and took a step closer. Every step took him closer to the next part of his life. His friends couldn't wait. They wanted to hop into adulthood, grins red with seal blood. Smoking would be after that, then the boats, then weekends in the pub. Bobby wished there could be a part in-between. Maybe there had been once, but adolescence was being eroded like soft rock. It was straight into adulthood now. No time for acne or moods.

Bobby held the club out in front of him. Pull well back and follow through. The seal followed the club with those damned eyes. It's not a fish, Bobby wanted to shout. I'm going to kill you with this, so stop looking at it like it's your best friend. At that moment, Bobby hated the seal. He hated it for being so stupid and trusting – and for tearing nets.

Bobby took several breaths, psyching himself up. It's an animal, he told himself. Vermin. One blow and it's over. Do it and belong. Don't do it, and be excluded forever.

The seal cub obligingly hoisted itself up on its front flippers, angling its conical head. The perfect target. There would never be a better target. Bobby wrapped both hands around the club, squeezing until the blood left his knuckles. He lifted the club high over his head...

It had been Babe's idea to set up a practice area. She was very bloodthirsty for a girl.

'Soldiers train for battle,' she explained, suspending the melon in a home-made string harness from a tree branch. 'So we should get ready to hunt the enemy.'

'Enemy?' said Bobby doubtfully.

Babe turned on him. Her name really didn't do her justice. Babe Meara was cynical beyond her years, and aggressive beyond her size. Several local lads had misjudged Babe's nature and were now walking with limps.

'Yes, Parrish,' she spat. 'The enemy. Seals. You should know better than anyone. Your own Dad's nets are taking the worst hammering. If I was you, I'd be diving off the rocks with a knife, hunting those vermin down.'

It was probably true. Babe had once tracked down the dog who ate her cat. Mister Toodles had been avenged with a half pound of steak stuffed with laxative pellets.

Babe took a magic marker from her pocket, drawing rough features on the melon. Round black eyes, a button nose and some whiskers.

Seán Ahern was a bit slow to catch on. 'What is that? A cat?'

Babe threw the marker at him. 'No, dimwit. Hello. Seals. We're hunting seals, remember?'

Seán rubbed his forehead. 'Oh yeah, seals. I see it now.'

His brother Seanie chuckled derisively. 'A cat. Dimwit.'

'Yeah, well, the nose threw me. It's kind of feline looking.'

Babe set the melon swinging, then backed up half a dozen steps taking a hurl from her belt. The hurl was two feet long with wicked looking metal bands criss-crossing the base. This particular hurl was banned from every playing pitch in the South-East, but Babe kept it around because it had a good weight and you never know when you might have to whack something.

She hefted the hurl like a midget ninja. 'The way I see it, the little sod is lying on the flat rocks, tearing up a length of net.'

Babe advanced slowly, walking sideways, hurl high behind her.

'So you come in slow. Never taking your eyes off the ball, melon, I mean head. He'll be moving about a bit so you have to try and anticipate.'

Bobby tried to grin along with the rest of them, but he had always had a good imagination. He could see the seal. For him the pale green melon had morphed into a water-slick, deep-brown head. The inked eyes sparkled and rolled. The ragged whiskers shivered in the breeze. The smile on Bobby's face was only skin deep.

Babe froze two steps from the target. 'This is the crucial point,' she whispered. 'This is when the seal could spot you. Then the bugger has two choices; he can run, or he can fight.' She twirled her hurl in one hand, it cut the air with a gentle whoosh. 'So you have to be ready for both.'

With speed honed by years of competition with taller people, Babe Meara took the final two steps, bringing her hurl slicing down at the swinging fruit. The first blow battered the melon from its harness of string. The second shattered it into a million soggy pieces before it hit the ground.

'Jesus,' blurted Bobby.

Babe grinned, green melon juice spattered across her forehead. 'Will you look at him. He can't even stomach someone killing a piece of fruit. You'll never be able to handle an actual seal.'

The others laughed, giving Bobby farmer slaps on the shoulder.

'Go on, Bobby, you egit.'

'Get a grip, Parrish. It's a melon. You, on the other hand, are a lemon.'

But Paudie, Bobby's closest friend in the group,

went deeper. 'Don't worry, pal. When the times comes Bobby Parrish will show us all. Isn't that right, Bobby. You'll show us.'

Bobby looked Babe in the eye, trying to salvage the situation. 'That's right. I'll show you.'

Babe held out her hurl. 'Why don't you start with a melon?'

As it had happened, Bobby hadn't had to go next. Paudie had grabbed the hurl and made a feck of the whole thing; prancing around, putting on a funny voice. Eventually striking his melon and stamping on the pieces. It was funny enough to make Bobby see that the melon was only a melon, no matter how many features Babe scrawled upon it. When his turn came, Bobby had driven the melon right out of its string harness. But it was only a melon, and it proved nothing.

Now things were different. This was a real seal in front of him, not a piece of fruit with a shell approximately the same size as a seal's skull. And the real seal's head was not swaying in a gentle, predictable arc. It was cocked to one side, staring fixedly at the club raised over Bobby's head.

Bobby was sure his father had been disappointed in him, though he hadn't said anything. Bobby had not been the first to bring in a seal's flipper. The smart money had been on Paudie, but Babe Meara had surprised them all by backing up her big mouth with action. She'd arrived on the slip two days after the melon incident with a brush stroke of red on her shirt and a flipper in her hand. She'd tossed the flipper onto the flags where Dick Parrish was gutting pollock.

'Pound please,' she'd said quietly.

Dick had handed it over. Babe had taken it, shoving it deep in her jeans pocket. No gloating. Not a word. Then Babe had gone home, and no one saw her for a couple of days. Bit of a chill, her mother said.

So now it was Bobby's turn. He had been doing his level best to avoid seals, but this little fella had more or less jumped out of the sea into his lap. The hereditary club was raised over his head and there was only one way for it to go. Down.

Bobby could feel the strain in his muscles. It was soon or never. Through the arch of his arms Bobby could see the dock's high wall. There were a couple of youngsters walking along the wall. Picking their way barefoot across the sharp patches of wind-scraped rock. When they reached the end, they jumped with squeals and splashes aplenty.

Bobby smiled. He could imagine the cold water folding itself around him. There was no better feeling. That moment of clear touch and sluggish sight. Then back into the world of air.

That's what I should be doing, he thought. I should be diving off the high wall, and hunting for baits and throwing fishing heads at girls. Not Babe obviously. Other girls. Not killing seals.

Kill the feckin' seal! said another part of him. Kill it and don't make waves.

It's vermin. Kill it! shouted Dad and Grandad and Babe and a hundred other voices in his head.

Bobby heard the two youngsters giggling in the distance, as they mounted the wall for another jump. He longed to join them. Throw down his family club, put on his old swimming togs and join them. But he couldn't. This summer a new phase of his life began. He was a young man now. Certain freedoms came with that but also certain responsibilities. He could stay up to watch action movies, he could cycle the five miles to the local disco, he could even bring the boat out on his own around the bay. But he also had to earn his keep, learn to smoke and kill seals.

It seemed as though he had been holding the club over his head for hours. The tendons in his arms sang like guitar strings. And the seal cub waited patiently for the game to begin.

I am stuck, thought Bobby. Trapped in this position. I don't want to do this, but I have to.

'You don't have to, son,' said a voice behind him.

Bobby turned, the club still raised above him.

His father was on the bank, squatting elbows on knees. His face was difficult to read. Maybe understanding was there. Maybe disappointment too.

'I do have to, Dad. I can too.'

Dick Parrish shifted his weight. 'I know you can son, but you really don't have to. Look.' Bobby's dad stood, shielding his eyes against the sun. He pointed a finger out into the bay.

Bobby turned seawards, and for several moments could see nothing out of the ordinary. Then he noticed a wedge of light among the wavelets. At first he thought it was a sun shimmer, until it switched directions three times in a second.

'Sprats,' breathed Bobby.

'Yes,' said his father. 'So the mackerel are coming in. All hands on deck. Let's go.'

The mackerel were coming in. For the first time in years. He was off the hook, for now. And maybe, if the fish stayed in for a few weeks, the bounty would be forgotten. Bobby lowered the club, glancing down towards the seal cub. But there was only a wet stain on the rocks, evaporating as Bobby looked at it. The seal knew the fish were coming and he would be there to greet them too.

Bobby hurried up the rocky incline after his father.

'I'll take the boat out,' said Dick Parrish briskly. 'I want you on the short wall with a line of feathers. Take a fishing box too, you'll need it.'

Bobby nodded. He could fish. Killing fish was easier than killing seals. People ate fish.

'Get your brother down here too,' continued Dick. 'He could do with a couple of hours away from the books.'

'Yes, Dad.'

They climbed over the stile into the quay itself. Nobody was walking anywhere. Everyone was scurrying.

This must have been what it was like before an air raid, thought Bobby. Everyone has a job to do, and maybe not much time to do it in. He took a moment to absorb what was happening before launching himself into the furore.

The quayside was thronged with locals searching for a good spot, like tourists around a luggage carousel. They carried lines and rods and containers of every kind. Buckets, washing baskets, pots and pans. All to be lowered into the spring tide. The sprats shimmered into the mouth of the dock like a sheet of sub-aqua chain mail, and behind them the silver-blue flash of a million mackerel, driving themselves greedily towards the dock. Once in, they would be trapped by the simple maze of quay walls, and only the lucky ones would escape. The locals had about three hours before the tide emptied the dock, then the remaining fish would be piled high on the sand, rotting quickly in the sun. Nobody wanted to eat rotting fish, so they had to be lifted fresh from the water. As many as possible. Later, the beached fish would be shovelled into salt and sold for fishmeal or bait.

Bobby's father clapped him on the shoulder. 'Enough gawking. Get a move on.'

'Right,' said Bobby, and set off at a run down the quay. Something made him stop and look back. His father was watching him go with a lost expression on his face.

You are not me, that look said. I thought you'd be a little me, but you are your own person. Dick Parrish cupped a hand around his mouth. 'Maybe we can talk later, about stuff. You know, things, seal clubbing, whatever.'

Bobby nodded. Was Dad prepared to let him be different then? Did he want to be different?

Bobby turned and ran towards their yard.

2

It Must Be her Age

by Mary Hooper

It Must Be her Age

As Mum and I went into the sitting room there was a sharp intake of breath from Aunty Nancy and a muffled 'Bloomin' heck!' from Uncle Jack, followed by, 'I do believe it's Dracula's daughter!'

Ignoring them, I stomped across the swirly carpet and slumped against the arm of the sofa. My outfit was much too tight to actually sit down.

I caught sight of myself in the sitting-room mirror.

I looked cool.

I looked Goth.

Chillingly Goth. I was wearing a black satin bodice, very tightly laced, and over it a long, black velvet dress slit open to the waist. Under the dress I was wearing thick, black fishnet tights and heavy boots, and I had a black cloak on top of everything else.

There was a silence while they took me in, then Mum said delicately, 'It's her age, you know. Thirteen. We think the best thing is to ignore this phase.'

'You're probably right,' said Aunty Nancy, shaking her head sadly at me.

'We just hope she'll grow out of it as soon as possible.'

'Does it speak?' Uncle Jack asked.

'I'm not deaf, you know,' I said, glowering at those present, who were discussing me like I was a piece of furniture with woodworm. 'I can hear *and* speak.'

'Just as well,' Uncle Jack said with a smirk. 'Because with all that black stuff around your eyes I don't suppose you can see.' He looked round for approval at this witticism, and Mum and Aunty Nancy tittered.

'But underneath she's still our little Felicity,' Mum said.

'Per-lease!'

'Or Flicka, as she likes to be called now,' Mum went on hastily. 'And of course, on the wedding day she won't be looking anything like she does today. Rest assured of that.'

'Well, I don't think she's going to like wearing what Joy wants her to wear,' said my aunt worriedly.

'Won't *she*?' I said. I'd always been taught that *she* is the cat's mother, whatever that meant. I think it probably means that to call someone 'she' in their hearing is rude, and in that case Aunty Nancy was being very rude indeed.

She peered at me. 'That lipstick is actually *black*, isn't it,' she said faintly.

'And what's that on its neck?' put in Uncle Jack.

'A tattoo,' I said. 'A tattoo of a spider's web.'

'Not a real one!' Mum said hastily. 'I wouldn't let her ruin her life like that. It's a wash-off one.'

'Wash-off, eh?' My uncle said. 'I bet that doesn't

see much soap.'

I pretended not to hear this, because I was dead embarrassed about having a wash-off tattoo. It was like having blond hair, or plastic spiders around your room. Which I did have, actually (the spiders, not the blond hair), because although, obviously, real ones would have been much more spooky and offensive, I was scared of them.

'She won't have that...that thing on her neck on the wedding day, will she?'

'Of course not!' Mum said.

'Thank goodness for that,' said my aunty, pretending to fan herself with relief.

I glowered again at her. It wasn't like she had exquisite taste or anything – I mean, what about the sickening orange-whorled carpet in her sitting room, the picture of horses running through waves hung on the wall, and the brown fluffy chairs? If anything was enough to make you shudder, *they* were.

We were visiting my aunt and uncle to talk about a wedding. Their daughter, my cousin Joy's wedding. Wedding of the Year, you'd think it was, from the fuss they were making. The thing was, if I'd been asked to be bridesmaid to anyone else I would have laughed scornfully, rolled my kohl-ringed eyes at them and shown them the door, but Joy and I were quite good mates.

She was about fifteen years older than me, so she'd baby-sat almost as soon as I was born and had taken me out in my baby-buggy all over the place. When I was about three (and too young to know any better) I'd thought that being a bridesmaid was a bit like being a fairy and had made Joy promise, pixie's honour, that I could be her bridesmaid when the time came. Now she'd met Gorgeous Gavin (that's what she called him; I thought he was a pillock) and it was all about to happen.

Two hours later I was in Joy's bedroom and listening to her talking to GG on her mobile. Well, I say talking, it was more giggling and little smacking kissing noises and long *mmmmms* and *aaaaahhhhhs* to the point of nausea. I mean, I do like boys, and have actually had one date in my life, but if the time ever comes when I spend an hour on the phone making kissing noises into it then you can lock me up and throw away the key.

When she eventually put the phone down she was all kind of starry around the eyes.

'I tell you, Flicka, he's one hell of a guy,' she said.

'Really?' I said disbelievingly, and then changed the tone and said it again, '*Really*?' only more smilingly and indulgently. After all, as her only bridesmaid I knew I should be supportive of her.

'Now,' she said, getting up, 'let's have a look at your bridesmaid's dress!'

As I tensed up, she went over to her wardrobe and flung open the door. 'I've bought one off the peg,' she said, and there was the swish of materials, the rustle of tissue. 'I knew you wouldn't want anything too fancy...' rustle...rustle... 'but the thing is, they are pretty fancy anyway. And a bit colourful. I mean, they just don't do them in black. But I don't think you'll mind this one too much.'

And with that she turned round, holding up a *thing* on a hanger. It was a pale lilac thing, lollopy, shiny and droopy, with a big sash bow in front, a frill of lace around the neck and another round the hem.

'Aah,' I said, quietly dying inside.

'Not too bad, is it?' she wheedled. 'And it'll only be for a couple of hours. Lilac is the theme colour of the wedding. Could have been worse. Could have been pink!'

Looking at the *thing*, I didn't think it could have been much worse, actually.

'And for your head,' Joy went on, bringing out a big ball of tissue, 'I've got this little snood. It's the same as mine – only mine's white, of course.'

She undid the tissue and brought out the thing called a snood. Snood by name, snood by nature. It looked as if it was something called a snood. It was similar to a hairnet, only thicker, with lilac flowers all over it.

I whimpered with horror.

'D'you want to try it on?'

'S'OK,' I said faintly. 'I'll wait until I wash my hair. Don't want to get wax on the…lovely flowers.'

'It's quite simple, isn't it? As I say, my snood's the same, but with white trimmings.' She beamed at me. 'God, I'm so excited and so looking forward to it. I can't wait!'

'Nor can I,' I lied. I felt some reassurance was due to her. 'Don't worry, I'll just tie my hair back on the day, I won't wax it or anything. And of course I won't wear this lipstick or the eye make-up.'

'Of course you won't!' Joy said. 'I know you won't let me down.'

'Only I think your mum and dad regard me as spawn of the devil,' I said. 'Your dad practically held a crucifix up in front of me as I came through the door.'

She laughed. 'Oh, take no notice. I was just the same at your age – and *they* were just the same about me. Once I was all dressed up and my dad made me take my dinner outside to the shed and eat it. Said he couldn't bear to look at me.'

I giggled.

'I was a punk. A kind of retro punk,' Joy said.

'The worst kind!'

'And one school holiday I had my hair cut into a full mohican.'

'I don't remember you like that!'

'Well, you were only about three.'

We grinned at each other. It seemed odd to think that someone who'd been cool enough to be a punk could actually look at this lilac *thing* with a matching *snood* and think they were halfway wearable. But, well, she was relying on me and she was my mate. And normal Goth service would be resumed straight after the ceremony.

The wedding day. It wasn't raining, that seemed to be the main thing. Rain had been the only topic of conversation in the family for weeks and months. Would it or wouldn't it on The Day? Long-term forecasts were discussed, seaweed was hung out to see if it shrivelled (or did something else, I forget) and the mums were constantly on the phone to the weather forecast place. Anyway, it wasn't raining, and everyone seemed to think this was a Very Good Thing.

Mum and I arrived at Aunty Nancy's at ten o'clock in the morning. The wedding wasn't until three, but Joy and I were going to the hairdressers first and, in view of this, I hadn't thought it was worth going along in anything but my full-on waxed hair. If they were washing it anyway, I didn't see the point of doing it twice.

'Oh!' Aunty Nancy said, staring at me in horror. 'She's still like it! Hair, make-up and all!'

'It's all right. It'll come off when she has her hair washed,' Mum said. 'She'll scrub up a treat.'

'Has it got the web tattoo?' I heard from Uncle Jack in the kitchen.

'No, it hasn't,' I said, stomping upstairs.

I went straight into Joy's room, barging in and expecting to find her a vision of loveliness in white tulle, but she was wearing a minging old dressing gown, had a white clay mask on her face and a pair of knickers on her head to keep her hair out of the way.

I averted my eyes from the lilac thing hanging on the door of the wardrobe. 'Here I am!' I said bravely. 'Come to be with you in your last hours of freedom.'

'Flick!' she said. 'I must give you your bridesmaid's present.'

I cheered up. 'I didn't know I was getting one of those.'

'Oh, it's traditional. The bride always buys her bridesmaid a memento of the day. Usually a little gold locket and chain to hang round her neck.'

The smile froze on my face as she got a box out of a drawer and handed it to me. It looked rather large for a gold locket and chain but I thought there might be a lot of wrapping paper around it.

'It *is* a necklace,' she said, and I feared the worst, but

when I opened it I found a *fantastic* studded dog collar. Black leather, with shiny silver studs. I'd wanted one for ages but Mum wouldn't let me have one.

Now Joy had bought me one, though, she'd have to let me keep it.

Not bad, I thought, for an hour or so of dressing up as a fairy.

'And if anyone knows any reason why this couple may not legally...' the Minister droned on, but no one stopped the ceremony or objected in any way (I think that only happens in films) so it looked like the wedding was going ahead.

I looked at my reflection in the polished silver vase on the altar.

I didn't look like me at all. Not the real me. I looked more dreadful than anyone could ever imagine: the lilac thing was flouncy, the snood was snoodish and my hair was in bouncy curls. Beneath the bouncy curls my face looked podgy and plastic because I was wearing pale lilac eyeshadow (to match the thing, natch) pearly pink lipstick and I had matching pink cheeks. What a *sight*. Joy looked no better; she seemed to be wearing a very large, decorative loo-roll holder and her snood had a veil that drooped around her face.

Leaning forward a little, I caught the reflections of the

first row of the congregation, and a right motley crew they looked. The men all wore grey suits that looked like cardboard and the women all wore vile flowery dresses. Yuk.

And then I saw a boy standing at the end of the front row. A quite decent-looking boy, from what I could see, except that he had a suit on and too-short hair and looked as if he might be a bit of a boffin. But not bad, though.

I pretended to brush down the lilac thing and turned slightly so that I could see him properly. And then I turned back quickly because he'd seen me looking, he'd grinned at me, and he was more than averagely fit.

'So…cousin of the bride, are you?'

He'd come up to me at the hotel afterwards, the boy, and started chatting quite easily.

I nodded. He had really gorgeous brown eyes. 'What about you?'

'Cousin of the bridegroom. My name's Lawrence.'

'I'm Flicka. So…does that make us cousins-in-law?' I asked.

'I guess so,' he grinned. 'You enjoying yourself?'

'Well…all this isn't exactly my scene,' I said, looking down at the lilac thing. 'I mean, I don't normally look like this.'

'No?' He raised his eyebrows. He not only had

gorgeous brown eyes, but also very long eyelashes.

'No! I was very nearly sick when I looked at myself in the mirror! Talk about a dog's breakfast!'

'That bad, eh?'

'I look so normal,' I said sadly. 'I look like everyone else!'

'Is that so awful?'

'That,' I said, 'is *chronic*.'

And then I realized how that sounded. How big-headed; as if I thought I was better than everyone else. (Which I actually did, in a way, but it is still just the wrong sort of thing to say to someone you quite fancy and you hope might be fancying you.)

I tried to make it better. I said, 'I mean, why does everyone have to be so conventional?' and then I realized that he – this Lawrence – was altogether conventional in every way and probably thought I was putting him down.

I floundered, and then I was saved, if that's the right word, by Uncle Jack appearing and doing his Bride's Father bit, clapping Lawrence on the shoulder and telling him not to bother with the likes of me but to go and get himself a glass of fizz. His actual witty words were, 'You wouldn't want to see it in the daylight! Talk about a vampire from beyond the grave!' as, ho-ho-hoing like a demented Father Christmas, he propelled Lawrence towards the bar.

'Well, thank you for seeing off the only good-looking boy in the place,' I muttered to my uncle's departing back, though really I'd probably done most of the seeing off myself.

Still, I thought to myself afterwards, through the wedding's cold roast dinner, interminable speeches and so-called funny jokes, he needn't have been put off quite so easily, need he? He could have come back again and we could have chatted some more and I would have tried to put things right. Pity, that. And though I looked for him when the embarrassing disco music started, I couldn't see him anywhere.

At eight o'clock Joy went to change, and I went along too. I'd promised everyone that I'd stay in the lilac thing all evening but – so unfortunate, this – I'd managed to tread on the hem and tear a big hole in it, so just had to change into the outfit I'd brought with me: my lovely little black satin mini with thick, knitted tights underneath. And in view of the occasion, I fixed a heavy black veil across my face and wore the special bridesmaid's necklace.

With the outfit, came my make-up. And my hair wax, and my beautiful heavy lace-up boots. Such a relief to have them all on again and, in spite of knowing that I'd scared off a really fit-looking boy, I felt better than I had done all day. As I applied my black lipstick extra generously, I consoled myself with the thought that he would have turned tail if he'd seen me Goth, anyhow. Someone as straight as he was would never have been interested in the real me.

Leaving Joy in the hotel bathroom I sauntered back down, pausing briefly on the sweep of the hotel stairs and hoping that someone would look up, see me and be rather horrified. It was then that my attention was caught by someone coming down the stairs from the opposite direction: a guy with thickly gelled hair in regular spikes across his head, wearing a black plastic top with thick fishnet sleeves, and an extremely cool pair of leather jeans with zipped openings all over them. He also had black eye make-up on, including mascara on super-long lashes.

'Hi,' he said.

It was Lawrence. 'H…hi,' I stammered.

And with me still gawking at him as we met where the stairs came together, he winked at me and took my hand. Then we walked down the rest of the way together.

'Blooming, blooming heck!' I heard Uncle Jack croak as we reached the bottom.

I smiled blackly at my Uncle. 'You'd better keep your neck well hidden,' I said. 'There's two of us now.'

And then we went to ask the DJ if he had any Siouxsie and the Banshees.

3

Dumb Chocolate Eyes

by Kevin Brooks

Dumb Chocolate Eyes

I never really liked Pete Cassidy. I spent a lot of time with him, and I suppose you could say we were friends, but I don't think we ever meant that much to each other. It was a friendship based on convenience more than anything else – we lived in the same village, we went to the same school, we both turned thirteen at the start of last summer...

But that was about as far as it went. I mean, we did stuff together, and sometimes we talked about things, but there was never anything more to it than that. In fact, looking back on it now, I don't think we ever really *knew* each other at all. It was just one of those things, you know?

He'd say to me, 'You wanna come round my place?'

And I'd say, 'Yeah...'

It wasn't supposed to *mean* anything.

It's hard to describe Cassidy as anything more than average – average height, average size, an average-looking face. His eyes were a bit on the weird side – kind of loose and lazy and chocolate brown – but apart from that, there wasn't anything remarkable about him.

His home, on the other hand, was unforgettable. It was a bungalow, for one thing, which I could never quite understand. I mean, what's the point of a house with only one floor? What's *that* all about? And, for another thing, all the rooms had really low ceilings, and they were all interconnected, like a maze of broad tunnels...and there were *loads* of them. It was ridiculous. It must have been like living in a warren. Whenever I went there, I could never work out where anything was, and I actually got lost once or twice...coming back from the bathroom, mostly – which was kind of embarrassing.

'Just going to the toilet,' I'd say. 'Back in a minute.'

Only I wouldn't be back in a minute, I'd be back in about half an hour, and then Cassidy would give me a really funny look, like – what the hell have you been doing? – and I wouldn't know what to say, so I'd just smile awkwardly and pretend that everything was OK. I don't suppose it would have mattered so much if we'd been better friends. I would have just told him that I'd got lost, and he would have laughed and called me an idiot, and I would have said it was his fault for having such a ridiculous house...and everything *would* have been OK.

Luckily for me, whenever I went round to Cassidy's place we spent most of our time in the garden, so I didn't have to worry too much about getting lost in his house. All I had to worry about was getting lost in his garden. It was a *huge* place. I mean, the first time I saw it, I couldn't believe it. Up until then, the only gardens I'd ever known were all pretty much the same – a rectangle of lawn at the back of the house, a few flower beds, maybe a couple of trees. But Cassidy's garden was something else. Cassidy's garden was a rambling wilderness that seemed to go on for ever: acres of land, dozens of sheds and porches, fields of wild grass and weeds, broken walls, stubs of statues, ponds, outhouses, cellars, basements...there was even a derelict swimming pool, hidden away at the bottom of the garden, all cracked and flaky and dead-eyed blue.

It was that kind of place.

A perfect mixture of paradise and hell.

Anyway, on the day I want to tell you about, me and Cassidy were hunting for rats in his garden. It was Cassidy's idea. He'd seen this rat the day before, scuttling around by the empty swimming pool, and he thought it'd be a good idea to catch it and kill it. I couldn't see the point myself. It was only a rat – why not just leave it alone? It wasn't doing any harm, was it?

'It's a *rat*,' Cassidy sneered. 'You don't leave rats alone.'

'Why not?'

'Because they're *rats*, that's why. They're pests,

they carry diseases...'

'What kind of diseases?'

'I dunno...rat diseases.'

'I've never heard of anyone catching a disease from a rat.'

'Yeah, well...what do *you* know?'

I didn't know how to answer that, so I just shrugged.

'Anyway,' he continued, 'this isn't just any old rat – it's a monster. I mean, it's *really* big – big as a cat.'

'Maybe it *is* a cat?'

'I think I know the difference between a cat and a rat.'

'Yeah?'

He looked at me then, and there was something in his chocolate eyes that told me I'd better shut up. This was his house, his garden, and if I didn't like the idea of killing a rat...well, I could always go home, couldn't I? And that was the funny thing, I suppose. I *could* have gone home. I could have said, 'OK, Pete, I think I'll be going now. I'll see you later – all right?' And it *would* have been all right. He wouldn't have cared. I wouldn't have cared. It wouldn't have meant anything to either of us.

So why did I stay?

I don't know...

I suppose it was just another one of those things. You know how it is – when you're at someone else's place, and they're doing something you're not quite sure about, and you know in your heart that you'd rather not be there, but you just can't bring yourself to do anything about it...?

Anyway, I didn't say anything to Cassidy, I just lowered my eyes and looked at the ground and waited for the moment to pass. And, after a while, it did. I heard him sniff a couple times, and when I looked up, he grinned at me and carried on talking as if nothing had happened.

'Yeah,' he said, 'and the thing is, when you see one rat, you always know there's going to be more. They breed like rabbits. There's probably *hundreds* of them around here...'

Breed like rabbits? I thought. First they're as big as cats, and now they breed like rabbits? What kind of rats are we dealing with here? I kept my thoughts to myself, though. I just nodded, like I knew what he was talking about, and then I quietly followed him around the back of the bungalow and down into one of the cellars.

I could never understand why his house had so many basements and cellars. They didn't seem to serve any purpose. As far as I could tell, they were mostly used for hiding away piles of rubbish – sacks of mouldy seeds, bags of solidified cement, coils of rusty wire, legless chairs, old bike frames...you know the kind of thing. It seemed a bit odd to me – keeping tons of useless old junk under your house – and I almost asked Cassidy about it once. 'Hey,' I was going to say, 'how come you've got so many cellars full of rubbish?' But I chickened out at the last minute, afraid of how he might react.

'You *what*?' I imagined him saying. 'What kind of stupid question is that? What's it got to do with you, anyway?'

Or maybe just – 'Uh?'

That was the thing with Cassidy, you could never quite tell how he'd react to anything. Sometimes you'd get a laugh, sometimes a grunt, and other times you'd just get one of his chocolate-eyed looks. Which is probably why I never asked him very much. It wasn't that I was *scared* of asking him things, it was more a case of – why risk a dirty look for the sake of some useless information? I mean, who cares what a cellar is for, anyway? It's a cellar, that's all. It's just a cellar.

And that's that.

So, anyway, there we were in this dusty old cellar – Cassidy searching around for rat traps, and me sitting on a pile of old newspapers, watching him – and I have to admit it felt pretty nice down there. Kind of cool and quiet, with that weird sort of underground feeling to the air – the kind of feeling that makes you think that the rest of the world doesn't exist.

Cassidy's face, as he rummaged around through the underground junk, was a picture of dumb concentration: narrowed eyes, furrowed brow, twitching nose. He looked a bit like a determined animal searching for something to eat.

'Where are you?' he kept mumbling to himself. 'Come on, where are you? I know you're in here somewhere...'

The more he searched – digging around, flinging things to one side – the dustier the air became, and after a while the whole cellar was clouded with a browny-grey haze. I could taste the dust in the back of my throat, and I could feel it clogging up my nose. It smelled quite pleasant, actually – kind of old and earthy and warm. As I sat there, breathing in the dust and the underground air, I could easily have closed my eyes and nodded off for a while.

But then I heard a harsh clatter of metal and a sudden cry of 'Gotcha!' and the momentary peace was broken. I looked up through the dust to see Cassidy burrowing down into a cardboard box, grabbing at something with both hands, and then he straightened up and turned towards to me with a triumphant grin on his face and a rusty old rat-trap dangling from each hand.

'Look at these!' he said excitedly, waving the traps at me. 'What d'you think? You ever seen anything like these before? Look at the *size* of 'em!'

'Yeah,' I agreed, 'they're pretty big.'

And they were. Imagine a mouse-trap – the old-fashioned kind that snaps down and chops off the mouse's head – and then imagine how it'd look if it was four times bigger…well, that's what Cassidy was holding in his hands. They were nasty, vicious, ugly-looking things.

'There's loads of them, look,' Cassidy said, bending down to the cardboard box again. 'I reckon there's about a dozen in here.' His eyes burned darkly as he lifted up the box. 'Come on, let's get out of here. You take the traps down to the pool and I'll go and get some bread.' He looked at me. I hadn't moved. 'Here,' he said, passing me the box. 'Come *on*, what's the matter with you? You wanna catch rats or not?'

I stood up and followed him out of the cellar.

I'm not sure what I thought about while I was standing by the empty pool, waiting for Cassidy to come back with the bread. I might have wondered what I was doing there – standing beside a derelict swimming pool with a cardboard box full of rat-traps at my feet – but I probably didn't. I probably just stood there, looking around, not really thinking about anything, just looking around and waiting for Cassidy to come back...

I really can't remember. It was just another moment, you know? Another moment, another day, another bit of life...

It didn't mean anything.

Why should it?

When Cassidy came back, half-running across the garden, he was carrying a bag of sliced white bread in his hand.

'This should do it,' he said, waggling the bread at me.

'Do rats like bread?' I asked him. 'I thought they liked cheese.'

'That's mice. Rats eat anything. They're hombivores.'

'Omnivores,' I corrected him.

'What?'

'Omnivores. Animals that eat anything are called omnivores.'

'I know - that's what I *said.*' He shook his head at me, like I was an idiot, then he opened the bag of bread and pulled out a slice.

I watched him as he knelt down and took one of the rat-traps out of the box. 'You've got to watch your fingers,' he told me, as he carefully baited the trap with bread. 'A friend of my dad's lost a thumb when he was baiting one of these.'

I raised my hand and wiggled my fingers in front of my face, trying to imagine myself without a thumb. It made me feel kind of shivery.

'Right,' said Cassidy, 'that's the first one done. Eleven more to go.'

I didn't set any traps myself, I just followed Cassidy around the garden – carrying the box, passing him the traps, preparing the bread, listening to what he had to say. I think he saw himself as the master rat-catcher...and he probably saw me as his apprentice.

'The thing is,' he told me, 'you don't want to put the traps too close together, 'cos rats aren't stupid. If one of them gets caught and the others see him lying there dead, they'll get suspicious. D'you see what I mean? They'll start to think that something's going on...'

'They'll smell a rat,' I suggested.

'Yeah,' he said, not getting it, 'they can smell things

from miles away. They can see in the dark, too. I told you, they're not stupid.'

He made it sound like a reason for killing them.

'How much bread have we got left?' he asked me.

I looked in the bag. 'Half a slice.'

'Give it here.'

I passed him the last piece of bread. Once again, he bit off half of it, chewed it for a while, then spat it out into his hand and rolled it into a ball.

'D'you want this?' he said, offering me the bit of the bread he hadn't chewed.

'Uh...no, thanks,' I told him.

'You sure? There's nothing wrong with it.'

I smiled and shook my head.

'Suit yourself,' he shrugged, popping the bread into his mouth as he carried on baiting the final trap. 'No point in waithting it.'

With the traps all set and laid out around the garden, we went inside to wait. It's hard to remember exactly what we did while we were waiting. I remember following Cassidy along the maze of tunnels to his room, so I guess we spent some time in there, but I don't know what we did. Not much, probably. I expect we just did what we usually did – hang around, look at stuff, maybe play a couple of computer games. Cassidy had one of those computer football games – not the action kind, but the kind where you're the manager and you have to pick your players and do all the transfers and stuff. He'd sometimes play it when I was there, which was pretty boring for me, because all he'd do was sit in front of his PC for hours searching through lists of players.

'What are you doing?' I'd ask him.

'Uh?'

'What are you doing?'

'I'm trying to buy a right-footed centre-back for less than half a million.'

'Oh,' I'd say.

And that would be that.

So, maybe that's what we did while we were waiting in his room. Maybe I sat there pretending to read a magazine while Cassidy tried to buy a centre-footed right-back for less than half a zillion...or maybe not. Like I said, I just can't remember.

But I'm pretty sure that after a while we went into the kitchen for biscuits and juice. Firstly, because that's what we usually did. And, secondly, because I remember seeing Cassidy's mum that day, and the only place I *ever* saw her was in the kitchen.

She was a funny little woman, Mrs Cassidy – kind of small and timid, she hardly ever said anything. Even when she was dishing out the biscuits and juice, she never said a word. She just scuttled around, smiling nervously. She seemed to spend a lot of her time doing that. Cassidy's dad was a scuttler, too. He was always dressed in blue overalls, and he always looked busy, but I never saw him actually doing anything. Cassidy had an older brother, too – an ugly thing called Wayne. I can't think of much to say about him. He had a fat belly and a fat head, and he thought he was smart, but he wasn't.

At least he didn't scuttle, though.

It must have been about an hour later when me and Cassidy went back outside to check on the traps. I still had the taste of cheap biscuits and watery orange juice in my mouth, and I was kind of desperate to use the toilet. But Cassidy was in a hurry – 'C'mon, c'mon, let's go...' – and I thought that if I *did* go to the bathroom I'd probably only get lost again. So I just gritted my teeth and followed Cassidy as he scuttled out into the garden. He could hardly wait to get to the traps. He was all flappy and over-excited, like a little kid on Christmas morning, and his eyes were blinking and twitching like mad. It was a little scary, to be honest. I was beginning to think there was something a bit psycho about him.

'How many rats d'you reckon we've got?' he said.

'Four? Six? Ten? What d'you think?'

I got the feeling he was talking to himself, so I didn't bother answering.

I could see most of the traps now. I could see Cassidy ahead of me, hurrying over to the nearest one.

'OK,' he was saying breathlessly, 'here we go, here we go...let's see what we've got.'

I saw him stop by the trap and look down at it, and I felt a kind of pause in the air, and then I was walking up beside him and looking down at what we'd done...and I don't think I'll ever forget it. Lying at our feet, its neck almost severed by the powerful trap, was a sparrow. One of its wings was sticking up awkwardly into the air, and its beak was wide open in a silent scream.

'Christ,' said Cassidy, looking around at the other traps.

And then he started laughing.

Every trap had a dead sparrow in its jaws. Twelve traps – twelve dead sparrows...their little brown beaks pearled with blood and their lifeless feathers ruffling in the breeze.

Something died in me, then.

I can't really explain it.

I just felt so bad...

So guilty, so stupid, so childish...

But I think the thing I felt worst about was my

ignorance. I'd known all along that we were trying to kill rats, but it wasn't until we'd killed twelve sparrows that I finally realised what we were actually *doing*.

I hated myself for that.

I hated what we'd done.

And I hated Cassidy and his dumb chocolate eyes.

He was still standing beside me, still pointing at the traps, still laughing and giggling and snorting like a madman...

I felt so sick.

I couldn't speak.

I turned around and walked away.

And that was the last I ever saw of Pete Cassidy. A couple of weeks later he was racing his bike down a hill in the village when he lost control and crashed into the path of an oncoming lorry. No one was to blame, it was just one of those things – an accident, a tragedy, a twist of fate...

Whatever it was, Cassidy died instantly.

And I still don't know how I feel about that.

4

Double Thirteen

by Eleanor Updale

Double Thirteen

THURSDAY 12TH FEBRUARY: 10.30PM

I know I promised myself I wouldn't start this diary till tomorrow. To mark the New Year. Not for everyone, of course. Just for me, and a few other poor souls who will be having their birthdays on Friday 13th. The unluckiest day of the year. I worked it out on the computer at school. It's actually quite rare. There are only two Friday 13ths this year. No year has more than three. Because of leap years you can go for ages without having your birthday on a Friday. It's not quite as unlikely as winning the lottery, but you probably only get about a dozen birthday Fridays in a lifetime. And I get one of mine tomorrow. That's in an hour and a half from now. I'll be thirteen years old on Friday 13th February. Double Thirteen. Double Unlucky.

It's a big thing, Thirteen. A teenager. Mum's already started joking about it. She was deliberately winding me up tonight. All I did was chuck my pudding in the bin when Chloe said it was loaded with calories.

'Oooh Oooh' said Mum, in that sing-song voice parents know will really hit you, 'Oooh Oooh.

Teenage angst!'

Well, of course I couldn't help stomping off and slamming the door after that. And they thought I'd gone. They thought I couldn't hear them laughing about me in the kitchen.

'Oh God,' said Chloe. 'Is that what it's going to be like after tomorrow? Seven years of flouncing around.'

I mean, what does she know about it? She's only eight. She's naturally skinny, like I was then. She doesn't know how it hurts. I know I'm fat. I can feel it all jiggling when I walk. That's why I don't run. It bounces then, and I can tell everyone's laughing at me. Even the ones who say I'm normal. But that's because they're looking at things like my horrible fingers – they're like knobbly sticks. Or my neck – you can see the bones in my shoulders. Disgusting. But you can't see my ribs. Not unless I breathe in. And not through a T-shirt.

I didn't want them to know I'd been listening outside the kitchen, so I came upstairs and had a bath before bed. But I was starving afterwards, and I couldn't get to sleep. So I went down and got myself some food. Some jelly and a dollop of chocolate mousse, with some of that spray cream on top. And that's why

I'm writing this diary. I realised as soon as I got up here what I was doing. I've read about it. It's bulimia isn't it? Bingeing. All part of the teenage thing. It's starting already. I've got to resist it. The bowl's on the floor here by the bed, and I'm not going to touch it. I'm not even going to look at it. I'm going to ignore it. So I've started this diary early to take my mind off food. To make a note that thirteen's come a few hours too soon. I'll try to write every day. To say what it's really like being thirteen. Then, if I have a daughter, I'll read it and remind myself. And I won't crack stupid insensitive jokes that only get people angry and lead them to do things that make them seem like typical teenagers, when they're not.

And anyway, this *is* going to be a big year for me. I'm not just going to be a thirteen-year-old. I'll be a thirteen-year-old who's birthday was on Friday 13th. I mean, I haven't got a hope.

I can see what it's going to be like. I've watched the others at school. I copy them. I mean, there are some things you have to live up to. You don't want to be a dork. People like Mum laugh about teenagers, but what they don't understand is that we don't have any choice. Does Mum want me to be a joke? I've got to do what the others do. I've got to be the same. Even though I'm different. Especially because I'm different.

I'm unlucky.

So maybe everyone at school is going to hate me anyway. Like they hate that boy in Year Nine with the violin. I mean, he practises *at lunchtime*. In one of those padded rooms on the music corridor. And his mum drives him everywhere. She parks right outside on the zig-zags. And she kisses him. There. In the street. Right in front of everyone. And at the Christmas concert she talked to the teachers loads. She called Mr Newman 'Colin'. Right there, where everyone could hear. And she let him tap her on the arm. We all saw it.

We were stacked up, balanced on chairs and blocks on the stage, waiting to sing that stupid medley of *Disney* songs. Well, I say sing, but of course I just mime. Mr Newman doesn't know. I'm better at miming that half the pop stars you see on TV. The violin boy and people like him sing. It's so embarrassing. At least I managed not to tell my mum about the concert until it was too late for her to change her shifts at work, so she couldn't come. I didn't have to worry about her showing me up by waving or something like that. But it was still a nightmare. I mean, *Disney* songs. What do they think we are? Children? They have no idea. Even if they realised our maturity, they'd just make it worse. Make us sing old pop songs or something. Like Year Ten at that concert. I mean, kids singing *Yesterday*! Even the botox-faced bloke who wrote it would realise how naff it is, sung by a school choir, sounding their 't's and rolling their 'r's. But Mr Newman was grinning like an idiot, thinking he was being cool or something. You can guess what he must have been like when he was at school. He'll have been like the violin boy. I bet his mum waved at concerts. Probably still does. Probably buys his clothes as well. And now there's her precious Colin, grown-up, and still a nerd, grinning and giggling like he's some sort of rebel for playing ancient pop songs in a school. It was embarrassing enough to *watch* Year Ten doing it. Imagine what it was like to be up on the stage. Child abuse.

So that's how bad things are now. That's life before Double Thirteen. It's that grim already, even without the teenage label and the bad luck I'll be getting from tomorrow. And I can imagine what that's going to be like. Here's a typical day in my new life. I'm going to write about how I think it will go. And by the way, writing this diary is working. I haven't touched the food in the bowl. So...

A DAY IN THE FUTURE: IN THE YEAR OF DOUBLE THIRTEEN

I get up. I've overslept because the crappy alarm clock Chloe gave me for Christmas has dead batteries. I mean, why doesn't Mum ever remember to buy batteries? It's not that hard. Anyway I hate that clock. It's got a picture of *BOIZNOYZE* on the face. The hands join on right over Jamie's nose. I think Chloe got it just to take the mickey. She knew I liked Jamie best – though the truth is I was already going off them, and I wasn't surprised when they broke up in January, after the row with their manager and that really terrible single that only got to number 31.

So, anyway, I'm already late, and I forget my geography homework (which I've actually *done* by the way, though Mrs Drysdale doesn't believe me, and puts me down for a detention to do it again on paper, which I'll have to stick into my book, so completely obliterating the evidence that I've had to do it twice). Because I'm late, I've missed the bus my friends get, and I'm stuck with a load of dorks, and I have to walk in the school gates with them. And Robbie, this gorgeous boy in Year Nine, sees me going in with them and thinks I'm their friend. And it gets worse, because the teacher gives me a Duty for being late, and it's handing out hymn books at assembly, and now Robbie thinks I'm some sort of God-Squadder too, so I know I'm finished there. And I'm sitting in Prayers just telling Jessica all this when the Head sees me talking, and makes me *stand up* in front of everyone and say what I was talking about. And I can't think what to say. So he gets all facetious and says (in that voice they use when they want to make you look really stupid), 'Perhaps you were commenting on the passage I was reading. What was it about?"

Of course I wasn't listening, so I think it's probably the usual stuff about God is Love, so I take a chance and say, 'Love, Sir.'

And everybody laughs. And I know I've picked the worst word I could have said, because the Head is into it now, and stays sarcastic, and says, 'You can discuss your love life in the playground! But not today. Today, you can sit outside my room in silence at break.' And he doesn't say it, but I know he's thinking, '*While everyone else talks about you in the yard. And they all think you fancy one of those dorks you were with this morning*'. And I won't be there to tell them all they're wrong now, and it's that stupid alarm clock with

BOIZNOYZE on that's to blame. And maybe I say that out loud by mistake, and someone hears and tells everyone that I still like *BOIZNOYZE*, even though I don't any more, and never really did anyway. And all morning people are humming that tune and doing the stupid hand movements from the video. And someone says how I know all the moves. And it's true I did learn them, but I only did them for a joke, and now they're making it sound as if I really liked *BOIZNOYZE*, and still do, even though everyone knows they're rubbish. And my bad luck continues, because Robbie from Year Nine is passing while this is going on and hears it all and gives me a patronising smirk. So I lash out at one of the girls who's laughing and, more bad luck, Mr Corley comes round the corner just as I accidentally catch her cheek with my ring (which I'm not supposed to be wearing, and wouldn't be, if I'd had time to remember to take it off when I was rushing to school this morning) and I'm marched back to the Head's office where he gives me a Very Serious Talk and makes me late for lunch, so I have to sit with the geeks who take in packed lunches, and I'm right next to the violin boy, who's actually got *home-made wholemeal sandwiches*, and I just want to die, because people will think I'm there on purpose, and that I fancy him.

So I'm finished anyway, but my bad luck gets even worse, and my period starts in Double Maths, and I don't realise until I hear people laughing behind me at when I stand up at the end of the lesson and there's a red patch on my dress. And they send me to the nurse, who goes all understanding, which is the worst thing of all, and she lends me a spare pair of school tracksuit trousers to wear home, so even people who don't know me, and haven't had the chance to get to hate me yet, think I like sport and that I'm in some kind of *team* or something, and so I'm finished with them too, and I haven't even got home to all the bad luck that waits for me there.

THURSDAY 12TH FEBRUARY: 11.15PM

So that's what it's going to be like for me in the year of Double Thirteen. But there's something else I've worked out. I'm going to get one extra bit of bad luck right at the end. This year is a leap year, right, so instead of my next two birthdays being at the weekend (so I can enjoy them at home, and don't have to go to school), guess what? The extra leap-year day pushes my fourteenth birthday to a Sunday. When I'm fifteen, it will be a Monday. A cold, winter, school Monday. It isn't fair.

*

Do you think the bad luck will stop a year from tonight, as I turn fourteen on that ordinary Sunday? Well, even if it does, I've got news for you. You know I said I'd checked out the calendar on the computer? Well guess when my next Friday 13th comes round? On my *eighteenth* birthday. So I'll enter adulthood unlucky. But it's worse than that. I know when I'm going to die. The day I'm eighty. It's too much of a coincidence. All my big dates are unlucky days. Thirteen, eighteen, eighty. It's meant to be. Somebody up there doesn't like me.

I'd better get some sleep.

11.25PM
No such luck. I'm still here. Still thinking about tomorrow. About the bad luck. Perhaps it has already started. I'll be so tired tomorrow I won't be able to do anything right, and everyone will hate me. I read in a magazine how your skin goes all grey and floppy if you don't get enough rest. Your eyeballs go dull. Maybe I'll get little red veins in them like Mrs McMichael, the one with the triplets. She told me she hasn't had a full night's sleep in two years. I saw her bending over the pushchair the other day. Her hair's gone all thin on top.

So I'll be tired and ugly.
And bald.
I'm turning off the light.

11.30PM
I'm still here. It said in the same magazine that if you write down the time every five minutes, the effort of trying to stay awake actually sends you to sleep. And when you wake up in the morning you can look at your notes and see exactly when you dropped off. Apparently insomniacs get more sleep than they think. They're just too tired to work it out or something.

So, it's 11.32 now. I'll be back at 11.37.

11.37PM
Still awake.

11.42PM
No luck yet.

11.50PM
Must have got a couple of minutes' shuteye somewhere there! But here I am, back again, and it's nearly midnight. Might as well stay awake now to see my birthday in. I'll just go to the loo, then come back to

bed and wait to see what bad luck the Fates have in store for me. What's the bet that the ceiling falls in at one minute past twelve?

FRIDAY 13TH FEBRUARY: 7PM

Well, I didn't have to wait for 12.01. Didn't even have to wait for Friday 13th to get officially started, as it turned out. Remember that dish of jelly and chocolate mousse on the floor? I didn't. Put my foot straight in it. Fell over and broke my ankle. Agony. But Casualty is quicker in the middle of the night. Remember that if you're ever planning an accident.

They all had a good laugh when they saw my date of birth.

'13 on Friday 13th!' said the doctor. 'I'm not superstitious, but you haven't wasted much time proving me wrong!'

Mum was nice though, considering there was jelly, chocolate, and cream all over the carpet, and she had to drive me to hospital in the middle of the night. And they let me choose the colour of my plaster cast. It's blue. Really cool. We dropped in at school this morning and everyone crowded round, and signed it with felt tips. I've got crutches too. Some of the girls looked at me with real envy. I've never had that before. It was great.

*

When Dad got home this evening the family gave me my presents. Chloe got me a new alarm clock. It's very designer. Stark chrome. Not a pop group in sight. No embarrassment. Batteries included. And I'm writing this on my new laptop. I've copied in all the stuff I wrote in my notebook last night, and now I'll finish off and put in a DVD. I'll be able to watch films in bed, with my foot up on a pillow. Mum's getting me a hot chocolate and the last slice of birthday cake. Even Chloe's being really friendly and helpful.

When the plaster comes off I'll have to go to physio every Wednesday afternoon. I'll miss Choir. They won't let me be in the concert at the end of term. I won't even have to mime.

Maybe Double Thirteen is special. Maybe one thirteen cancels the other out. Anyway, so far it doesn't seem so bad after all.

5

What I Did in my Holidays, by Sam Greenside (Class 3C)

by Paul Bailey

What I Did in my Holidays, by Sam Greenside (Class 3C)

What did I do in my holidays? I'll tell you. I looked after my mother.

In July, when school broke up, I still had a dad. Actually, he was as much a friend as he was a father. I called him Nick, because that's what he wanted. Mum wouldn't dream of letting me call her Sylvia – it's wrong, she says, for a son to talk to his mother in that way. That's why he was Nick to me when we went to the football on Saturday afternoons, and when he took me for a spin in the Merc, or when the two of us were together, Nick and Sam. But it was Dad in the house as long as Mum was around – Dad this, Dad that, and Sam, son. We had a laugh whenever Dad said 'Sam, son', and Dad would warn me to watch out for Delilah.

'She'll chop your hair off, Sam, as soon as look at you.'

Delilah's in Chapter Sixteen of the Book of Judges in the Bible, in case you don't know. Nick read the story of how she made Samson lose his strength when I was little, saying it was only a story and not to be confused with the truth.

'Read the whole Bible before you grow up, Sam,

son. Then you can blind those so-and-so Jehovah's Witnesses with science when they come pestering you with their pamphlets.'

Nick didn't like people who tried to press their opinions on you.

'I've got my views and they've got theirs,' he used to say. 'Keep an open mind, though. You will learn something new every day if you do.'

Nick was alive on July 20th, but the next day he was dead. Yes, dead. I saw it happen. He was talking to me about the trip to Spain the three of us were going to take. He was smiling at the thought of two weeks in the sunshine. I saw his smile go and his hands clutch his stomach and heard a noise come out of his mouth I've never heard before. It was like the cry of a wild animal caught in a trap. I swear that's what it sounded like – not human, if you follow me.

'Sam' was all he could say after that. My name was the last word he spoke.

I phoned for an ambulance and tried to reach my mum on her mobile, but it was switched off. The paramedics told me what I knew already, because I'd checked his pulse and heartbeat. I did what I could, and it wasn't enough, to save him.

Of course, I was upset inside. I don't have to tell

anyone how much I was choked. Well, I was, but it was as if I had a voice in my head warning me to stay cool. Stay cool, Sam, whatever you do. Stay cool for Mum's sake.

That's what I did. I'm not boasting, but it's what I had to do. I sat all alone in our house waiting for Mum to come home. Correction – I couldn't sit still. I moved from one room to another, but not into their bedroom. No, that was definitely out of bounds. The bedroom was *their* room, if you see what I mean.

I tried Mum's mobile again, but it was still switched off. Where was she? What was she doing? I thought of phoning Gran but decided not to. Nick was her only son, just as I'm his, and it didn't seem right for me to be the one to tell her. It had to be Mum was what I reckoned.

But in the end it turned out to be me, Me, Mr Mature and Grown-up at the ripe old age of thirteen years, three months and six days. Correction – six and a half days. It went like this. I was in the kitchen, still waiting for Mum to come home, thinking that I never wanted to eat or drink again, when the doorbell rang. At first I just let it ring But it was Gran, I could see through the glass panel.

'Surprise, surprise,' she said. 'I hoped someone was

in. Give me a big, big kiss, Samuel.' That 'Samuel' was Gran's regular joke. 'I have some good news.'

What could I say? What I did say was, 'Really Gran?'

'Let me come inside and I'll tell you.'

We walked down the hall, arm in arm, and then Gran told me she'd come into some money. My grandad, who died when I was just a baby, had been a prisoner of war in Japan and now, fifty years on, she was receiving compensation he should have had when he was alive.

'Ten thousand lovely pounds, my darling. What can I buy you?'

What could I say? What I did say was, 'Oh anything, Gran.'

'That's not like you. You always know exactly what you want. Where's Mum? Where's your dad, Samuel?'

'Mum's shopping somewhere, I think.'

'I might have guessed.'

I had to speak. I couldn't not say anything.

'Dad's at the hospital. St Luke's.'

'Why? What's the matter with him?'

'He's dead, Gran.'

'Is this a joke, Sam? Because if it is—'

'It's not a joke. It's true. Dad's dead.'

'No.' That's all Gran said. 'No, no, no.'

I made her sit down. I brought her a glass of Nick's 'medicinal' brandy and told her exactly what had happened. I don't know how I got the words out, but I did.

Then we both said nothing at all for a long, long time.

The sound of Mum opening the front door made me start. She had eight shopping bags – 'My holiday outfits,' she explained – and I took most of them from her.

'Nothing too expensive, Sam. I haven't been *that* extravagant. Nothing that's going to make a big dent in you father's bank balance.'

Her voice sounded brighter than I had ever heard it.

'Shall I make us some tea? I'm absolutely gasping I have to say.' She laughed. 'Serious shopping can be very tiring.'

'Gran's here.'

'Oh, that's nice.'

'Mum, I've got news. Bad news.'

'Is it to do with school?'

'No, Mum.'

'What on earth is it? How bad is bad, Sam?'

'Very.'

We stared at each other.

'Dad's dead. He died in front of me this afternoon.'

'No, he didn't. Of course he didn't. You're making this up.'

Is my mother really this stupid? I found myself thinking. Can she actually believe that her son would invent something so cruel?

'I've made nothing up. I wouldn't. I couldn't. It's the truth.'

We were only allowed to see him after the doctor had performed the post-mortem. We were told – or rather, Mum was told and she passed it on to me – that he had advanced liver cancer.

'He never said he was in pain. He must have been in serious pain if it was advanced. Oh, God, Sam – he must have carried on as if nothing was the matter with him. He was pretending. Pretending to his wife and son that he was healthy.'

Mum talked in this way for days on end. I listened. She blamed herself for not being more sensitive and for not noticing that her husband was seriously ill.

'Why his liver, Sam? He hardly touched alcohol. He drank the odd beer or wine on special occasions, but he wasn't a drinker like his father. It isn't fair. It just isn't fair.'

I listened, even when she said the same things over and over again. And as I listened, I realised I was doing something very important for her and for me. If there were no listeners, the world would be a worse place than it is already. The thought came to me as I sat there, holding her hand when she'd let me, that I was suddenly growing up fast. It wasn't the way I wanted to grow up, but there it was. I knew I was as upset as Mum, but I was the one who had to give her comfort. I'm not boasting. I had to comfort her, nothing more or less.

It was the same on the day of the funeral. It was me who phoned the caterers to supply the food and drink for our relatives and family friends at the reception afterwards. Mum said she couldn't cope, and I said that I would. And it was me who did most of the handshaking before the service, which was a very simple one. I had to brief the vicar about the kind of man that Nick was – successful in his business and the best dad I could have hoped for, as well as a loving husband. I chose *Jerusalem* for everyone to sing at the end, because it was Nick's favourite. 'I will not cease from mental fight,' – that was the line that always got him, he said. 'Don't cease from mental fight, Sam,' he'd say, and I'd reply 'I won't, Nick. No chance. You can depend on me.'

Mum keeps worrying about how we'll cope, but I know we will. We have to. It's that simple, or that complicated. I'm still listening. Somebody has to listen, and for the moment that person is Sam Greenside, whose summer holiday this year took an unexpected turn. We didn't go to Spain, even though Nick would have wanted us to and Mum bought all those outfits. It didn't seem right, in the circumstances, Mum said.

Mum mustn't see what I've written. She'd think I was being big-headed, which I know I'm not. All I've done is put down the truth. I had to keep my tears to myself, for her sake.

'Your mother's doing enough crying for all of us,' Gran said, and then she apologised, wishing that her tongue had been bitten off, but she didn't mean it nastily.

I hope the time to laugh and smile will come again soon. But there's a part of me now that will be serious for ever. I watched my own father die and my name was the last word he spoke. You can't alter that. The scene will never leave me.

So that's what I did in my holidays. A year from today I'll be writing something different, something a bit funny – ha-ha and peculiar, perhaps – with any luck. There is really nothing more to tell you.

*

Evaluation:
Thank you for sharing this with us, Sam. You are very brave and honest. I should be genuinely pleased if you could read this essay out in class, but I understand perfectly if you don't feel up to it. Well done.

Joan Fleming

6

Hey! This is Me!

by Jean Ure

Hey! This is Me!

When I was little, I desperately wanted to be nine. Goodness knows why. I guess I thought that once I was nine, things would change. *Something would happen.*

Well! So I got to be nine and things went on just the same as always. Nothing whatsoever happened, except that I fell out of a tree and broke my arm. Hardly what you would call momentous.

After that, I transferred my allegiance to thirteen. Thirteen was the age to be! Things would happen when I turned thirteen.

So I turned it, and they did.

To begin with, it seemed like thirteen was going to be disappointingly no different from eleven or twelve. Or even nine. It got off to a *really* bad start with Mum and Dad giving me presents that were so naff I could hardly believe it. Not even Mum could choose presents that naff – surely! They gave me a ridiculous sparkly top that I might have worn when I was about *two* but now wouldn't be seen dead in, plus a pair of trainers that I'd sighed and swooned over a few months back, but which were now so past their sell-by date that they should have been recycled. Nobody, but nobody, wore trainers like that any more.

Mum, needless to say, was all eager and beaming, so

I tried my best to look pleased and make happy noises like 'Ooh! Trainers! Ooh! A top!' but I could tell I hadn't convinced her 'cos her face immediately fell. Mum is *so* transparent; she doesn't have any pride. I was sorry to disappoint her, but I was disappointed, too! I mean, hey, this was my birthday, right? Birthdays come but once a year. You spend weeks looking forward to them, then people buy you stuff you don't even want. Why couldn't they just have given me the money? Then I could have chosen for myself. You don't want your mum doing it for you when you're thirteen! 'Specially not my mum. She would be the first to admit she has no dress sense.

Well, anyway, from that point on things just went from bad to worse. Dad complained that I'd become a right little madam.

'Very hoity toity! You'd better watch that attitude of yours, miss.'

Mum, sticking up for me as usual, said that it was 'just the age she's at.' According to Mum, thirteen is a *difficult* age.

'She's not a child, she's not an adult…she's finding her way. Just give her a bit of breathing space.'

Dad grumbled and said he'd give me more than that if I didn't change my tune. 'She'll get the rough edge of my tongue!'

If it hadn't been for Mum jollying us along, me and Dad would almost certainly have come to blows. I do love Dad, and I don't enjoy quarrelling with him, but he just has no idea what it is like to be thirteen in the modern world. Even when I had my party, which I shared with my best friend Carrie, Dad had to leave the room because he couldn't bear to see me dancing *with a boy*. A boy! Shock horror! He said afterwards that it wasn't the dancing he minded, it was 'all the other stuff'.

I said, 'What other stuff?'

'He had his hands on your bum!' roared Dad.

Oh, dear! Even Mum had to laugh. But as the weeks went on, the situation became positively fraught. We had regular bellowing sessions.

'No child of mine is going anywhere dressed like that!' (Skirt too short, top too skimpy.)

'I thought I told you to be home by 8.30?' (8.35, I kid you not.)

'Tamsin Walters, you go and wash your mouth out…using language like that!' (Totally harmless word employed by all and sundry. Well, certainly at my school.)

Sometimes Mum defended me, sometimes she didn't. But in the end, I have to say, it was Mum who upset me far more than Dad. Everybody who's thirteen has problems with parents who nag and lay down stupid rules; I could cope with that. What I couldn't cope with was Mum turning up at school looking like she'd pulled her clothes out of a garbage dump. Well, OK, maybe that's a bit of an exaggeration, and I'm aware that it makes me sound totally horrible. I know there are people that would say it is extremely small-minded to care about such things, and that clothes are not important, but I beg to differ! I think clothes are hugely important. I think that they are statements to the world. 'Look! Hey! This is me!' I bet if two people went for a job, and one was smart and well-dressed and the other was just a frowsy mess, I bet I know who the job would go to. So you *can't* say that clothes are not important. Not if you live in the real world.

It was the summer fete when Mum put me to shame. We were all there, standing behind our stalls (me and Carrie were on soft toys) when in the distance I saw this big pink shape wobbling towards me. Gulp! It was Mum. I just nearly died. She was wearing her *tracksuit.* To our school fete! For everyone to see!

I said, 'Oh, God!' and covered my eyes.

'What's the matter?' said Carrie.

I groaned. 'Look what my mum's wearing!'

Carrie is too nice to make rude remarks about

anyone's mum; but she is also a very honest sort of person.

'I expect it's comfortable,' she said.

'She looks like a big pink jelly!' I wailed.

'Well, at least she's here,' said Carrie.

Carrie's own mum hardly ever comes to school functions. (Mind you, when she does, she turns up looking like a movie star.)

'*And*,' squealed Carrie, 'she's going to buy something! Aren't you, Mrs Walters?'

'Of course I am,' said Mum, who'd reached our stall just as Carrie said this. 'Must support the cause!'

'That is just *brilliant*,' said Carrie, as Mum went on her way clutching a bright yellow duck and a hand-knitted Tigger. 'Your mum is so lovely!'

I agreed that she was. Because of course she *is*. But then, guess what? She had to go and stop at the stall next to ours, which was being run by two particularly obnoxious girls that are, unfortunately, in our class. Dana Wilkinson and Arleen Petrie. I would rather Mum had stopped anywhere but there! Afterwards, almost before she was even out of earshot, I heard Dana's voice: 'What was *that*?' To which Arleen giggled and said, 'Candy floss on legs!' OK, so now I'm going to admit something that quite honestly I would far rather not admit, because I hate myself for it, but like it or not it happens to be true. Instead of feeling angry on Mum's behalf, I just felt utterly and completely covered in shame. My cheeks grew crimson and I wanted to scream out, 'She isn't *my* mum! She's nothing to do with *me*!' Carrie must have guessed how I felt, because she squeezed my arm and whispered, 'Take no notice. They're just rubbish!'

All very well, but easier said than done. Taking no notice, I mean. It is terrible to feel ashamed of your own mum. It's especially terrible when, like me, you're adopted and have been told over and over that you are the *very best present* your mum ever had. Well, and your dad, too, of course, but in my case it is always Mum who says these things. Poor Mum! She would have been so hurt if she had known how I was feeling. But I still couldn't stop feeling it; and, as the day wore on, I even started to build up a great simmering mass of rage. Not against those obnoxious girls, but against Mum herself. How could she do it to me? She'd made me a laughing stock! The girl with the big pink mum…

Two weeks later, it was Year Eight Open Evening. Desperately I tried telling Mum that there really wasn't any need for us to go, but she was horrified at the suggestion.

'Of course we're going to go!'

'Well, maybe Dad should come, for a change. It's

not fair, you always having to make the effort.'

'It's no effort,' said Mum.

'But there isn't any *point*,' I said. 'Just a few grungy old teachers standing around—'

'Well, I want to talk to some of those grungy old teachers,' said Mum. 'Don't worry! I won't wear my tracksuit.'

Heavens! Did that mean she'd heard? Dad, who can be quite protective where Mum is concerned, said she could wear what she liked. 'It's not a fashion show, is it?'

'No, but I'll put on a dress,' said Mum. 'Something suited to the occasion.'

I do believe Mum tried; I really do. But in some ways the dress was even more of a disaster than the tracksuit. At least Mum looked like Mum in the tracksuit. The dress was like a sort of…tent. A big shapeless bell tent, covered in purple flowers. I just prayed that it would be cold in the school hall and she would keep her coat on, but no such luck. It was boiling hot. I was in agony all the time we were there. I couldn't remember being in agony on previous years, but I supposed it was something to do with being thirteen and more conscious of the image that Mum presented. I think perhaps you don't care so much when you're only eleven or twelve. Growing older does have its drawbacks.

Halfway through the evening I left Mum talking to Miss Pringle (Geography. My worst subject!) and went off in search of Carrie. Her mum usually turns up for Open Evening, and there she was, looking like a movie star as always.

'Your mum is just *so* glamorous,' I told Carrie.

'Yes,' Carrie sighed. 'She keeps on at me to watch my diet.'

'Isn't she scared of anorexia?' I thought all mums were scared of anorexia, but Carrie said glumly that her mum was more scared of spare tyres and rice pudding thighs.

'Yes, and *someone's* mum has come in fancy dress!'

I spun round. It was that hateful girl, Dana Wilkinson.

'What are you talking about?' said Carrie.

'Oh, not *your* mum. Someone else's mum. I like the purple flowers!'

'Just shut up,' said Carrie.

'What's your problem? I'm paying a compliment.'

'You're being nasty!'

'I'm not being nasty. I was just saying, about her mum—'

Before I could stop myself, I had blurted it out: 'She's not my mum!'

It was, like, sudden, total silence. Just for a split second. Then Dana went, '*Oh?*'

And Arleen, who'd popped up at her side, went, '*Oh?*' And then they both went, '*Since when?*'

I snapped back, 'Since I was born! Sh—'

I was about to say that she was my adoptive mum. Not my *birth* mum. But I became aware of Carrie tugging urgently at my sleeve.

'Tam! Shut up!' And then, breaking into a big bright beam, she cried, 'Hallo, Mrs Walters!'

Mum was right on top of us. Oh, God! This time she'd have heard for sure. Half the room would have heard. I know my voice is abnormally loud because my gran tells me that it is. Whenever I go and visit her she claps her hands to ears and says, 'Blot out the raucous voice!' And *that's* when I'm just talking normally.

As I said before, my mum is not one to hide her feelings. Not as a rule. If she's happy she laughs, if she's sad she cries, and if she's hurt she lets you know it. But that evening she was, like, truly dignified. In spite of the purple flowers. Calm as could be, she said, 'Hallo, Carrie.' It was the rest of us who squirmed and wriggled. Poor Carrie had gone bright pink; even Dana and her stupid friend were looking uncomfortable. As for me, I just wanted the earth to open up and swallow me. When will I ever learn?

Next day, Carrie asked me if Mum had said anything. 'About – you know! Last night.'

I said no, she hadn't said a word.

'Maybe she didn't hear?' Carrie suggested somewhat half-heartedly. I agreed, even more half-heartedly.

'You know what you were saying,' said Carrie, 'about her not being your real mum…?'

'Yes, but I didn't mean it,' I said. 'I was just embarrassed 'cos of her showing me up like that.'

'She didn't show you up,' said Carrie. 'Nobody cares what other people's mums look like!'

I thought that it was all very well for Carrie. *Her* mum had once been mistaken for Nicole Kidman. Mine just got laughed at.

'It isn't fair!' I said.

'Who would you have for your real mum,' said Carrie, 'if you could choose?'

'*Birth* mother,' I said. 'That's what they're called.'

'OK, so who would you have?'

I thought, Nicole Kidman! But I didn't say it, as it would have seemed a bit superficial. So I just said that I would like someone who was smart and well-dressed.

'Mmm…but then they mightn't be as nice as your mum,' said Carrie.

I said, 'Why shouldn't they be? There's no reason someone can't be nice *and* well-dressed.'

Carrie said she supposed not.

'*Your* mum's nice,' I said.

'Yes,' said Carrie. 'But your mum's kind of…cosy.'

I told Carrie that I didn't want a mum who was cosy. I wanted a mum I could be proud of! A mum I could go places with. A mum that hateful girls like Dana Wilkinson wouldn't laugh at. I didn't see how that was so unreasonable.

When I arrived home that afternoon I got a big surprise: Mum'd had her hair cut off. She'd had it cut *really short*.

'What do you think?' she said as soon as I walked through the door.

I felt my mouth drop open idiotically.

'Don't you like it?'

I swallowed. 'I expect I will when I've got used to it,' I said.

Well! I mean. It was quite a shock, seeing Mum like that. As long as I could remember her hair had been like a sort of tangled thicket.

'I thought it might make me look younger,' she said.

I assured her that it did (trying hard to sound convincing) and went off to my bedroom to listen to some music and get myself in the mood for Maths homework. I'd only been there about two minutes when there was a knock at the door and Mum appeared.

'Tamsin,' she said, 'I've got something for you. Here.' She handed me an envelope.

I said, 'What is it?'

'There's a photograph,' said Mum, 'and a letter. Written by your birth mother. She got in touch a couple of years ago, wanting to know if she could meet you. I said that when I felt you were ready, I'd give you the option. I was going to wait till you were older, but – well!' Mum gave a little sad smile and touched self-consciously at her shorn hair. 'You're thirteen, and you seem a bit…unsettled. I thought perhaps it might help. You don't have to decide immediately, but if you feel you'd like to meet her, we can arrange it.'

Mum went off, leaving me alone with the envelope. For a few minutes I just sat there, turning it over in my hands. It's a bit of a creepy feeling, knowing that you are about to look at a photograph of the woman who gave birth to you. I'd been told one or two things *about* her, like she was still at school when she'd had me, but I'd never seen a photo. Suddenly I was scared and wasn't sure that I wanted to. It could be the hugest disappointment of all time! You are always reading these stories of adopted kids who fantasise about their real parents being rich and famous; and then when they finally trace them they are junkies, or dropouts, or just generally sad people. Or even just depressingly *ordinary* people. I didn't want a mum who had two kids and lived in a boring flat on a boring street with a boring job!

But if I never looked, I would never know.

Deep breath. I took out the letter. Address – London. SW19. Was that good? I didn't know. I don't know London!

It was only a short letter. She said how she so often thought of me, and wondered how I was doing. She's a banker now and works in the City. Wow – posh! She said she would love to meet me one day, if such a thing were possible.

I wondered how old she was? I counted on my fingers. 28? 29? Still young! Imagine having a mum who is in her twenties.

At last I am brave enough to look at the photograph. Caroline Allsopp; that was her name. She is slim and blond. So am I! I take after her! Her clothes are to die for. Just a shirt, and jeans, and boots, but you can tell at a glance they're quality. This is my mum! My real mum! And if I want, I can go and meet her…

I never got to do my Maths homework. Instead, I lay on top of the duvet, dreaming about Caroline Allsopp. I dreamt about what I would wear, when I went to see her. I dreamt about how she might come along to a school function. (Dana Wilkinson, eat your heart out!) How I might even go and stay with her, in SW19. How we might jet off to America together…

But then – I don't know how it happened – I started having second thoughts. Maybe it was the sight of Mum, all vulnerable with her short hair, when I went down later to have dinner. Dad was obviously as stunned as I had been.

'What's all this?' he was asking. 'What have you done to yourself?'

I saw Mum's lips tremble.

'She's had her hair styled,' I said. 'Don't you like it? I think it's great! It makes her look ever so much younger.'

Mum said, 'It's all right, luvvy. You don't have to pretend.'

'No, I mean it!' I followed Mum out to the kitchen, to help carry things in.

'Have you come to any decision?' said Mum.

'You mean about…the meeting?'

' I can speak to your dad. We can set it up for you.'

'The thing is,' I found myself saying, 'I – I'm not quite sure I'm ready for it yet.' The words came out in a gabble. 'I think I'd rather wait a bit. Till I'm older, you know? Like maybe when I leave school, or something. D'you think?'

'Oh, Tammy,' said Mum, 'it's not what I think. It's what you think.'

I said, 'Well, that is what I think.'

'Are you sure?'

Was I sure? I hadn't been, when I came downstairs. When I came downstairs I'd still been fantasising about America. Me and my young mum… But then I had looked at my real mum, 'cos this *was* my real mum, the mum who'd loved me and cared for me and put up with my moods and my tantrums all these years, and – yes! I was very sure.

'You're not just saying it?'

'I don't just say things,' I said. 'I SHOUT them!'

'You're telling me,' said Mum.

'What I'm telling you…' I hurtled across the kitchen and threw my arms round Mum's neck. 'What I'm telling you is, I LOVE YOU!'

7

bad language

by Marcus Sedgwick

bad language

i don't see what the problem is. but then that says it all. because the trouble is i don't see things the way they do.

but i guess i should know by now. sooner or later someone decides to give me a hard time.

i should have learned. it happens often enough.

might be a teacher, might be some other kid.

first time i learnt to keep my mouth shut was in maths.

hargreaves takes maths. likes to think she's smart. tried to scare us with some tricky stuff. so she put up a tidy list of quadratics on the board. i want those finished by the end of the lesson, she said, and went over to her desk.

when she sat down she looked up and saw me with my hand in the air.

what is it, gray? she asked.

i've finished them, miss, i said, what should i do now?

if looks could kill...

there were a few sniggers from behind me but wargraves glared and that was that.

don't be facetious, gray, she said, get on with your work.

but i have finished them, i said.

moreglaze looked at me then, and it was not a nice look.

very well, then. number one, she said.

x equals 8, i said.

there was a little laughter, but it soon stopped.

she, poorgaze i mean, didn't say anything for a moment. then she said, correct. number two?

x equals 3, i said.

she didn't have to say i was right.

number three?

x equals plus or minus 2, i said.

it went on like that. she barked out the questions at me and i answered them all. she started getting faster and faster. it was interesting to watch. then she started to get angry, and was practically shouting the numbers out at me, and every time i answered it only made it worse.

eighteen! she said.

x equals 11.

nineteen!

x equals 7.

she spat the questions out, number after number, and i kept on giving her the answers, which is what you might think she wanted. but you'd be wrong. that was the first thing i learnt that day. that sometimes what people ask you for is not what they really want.

she didn't want us to solve the quadratics, she didn't want us to learn. she wanted to fill the time until the end of the lesson.

she got to the end of the list, and only at that point did i notice how quiet the class was. all the giggling had stopped. no one said anything. harddays just stared at me, so i looked away, and saw that everyone else in the class was staring at me, too.

i thought maybe they'd have liked that, because it was sort of funny and it had made an unpleasant teacher look a bit silly. but i was wrong. no one was smiling at me. i heard some boy whispering behind me.

freak, he said.

freak.

so that was the second thing i learnt. keep your mouth shut. now i act dumb in class. i get things wrong on purpose, make mistakes, and pretend i'm not listening. that kind of thing. teachers think i'm stupid, but it's easier that way. less trouble.

but sometimes that's not enough.

sometimes even walking somewhere gets you in trouble.

most of the time i get away with it, but there was this time last year when someone caught me.

the thing is, i don't like to walk the same way twice.

not in the same day. And if i really have to go the same way twice in the same day, then i go three times, or five, or seven.

don't ask me why, i don't think there's a reason.

i call it evenshapehate. because that's how i see it in my head.

so i was walking to the science block, counting my steps to make sure they were odd, and realised i'd already been that way once that day, so i turned round and went back to the start of the path, to make it three times. but someone saw me do it.

just so you know, it was one of the boys in my class, one of the ones who really hate me, but i don't want to say his name. and actually, it doesn't matter, because they're all the same.

what are you doing? he said. he was sort of sneering, his face was ugly because of the way he sneered at me.

i didn't say anything to start with, i couldn't make any words come out of my mouth.

what are you doing today, freak? he said. forgot where you were going?

that sort of helped me really, because there was no way i could have explained to him about evenshapehate, even if i had wanted to.

yes, i said, forgot where i was going.

stupid freak, he said, but when i didn't reply he left me alone.

i don't talk to anyone much, really, because it usually goes wrong. it's safer not to start things that could go wrong. and the one time i tried to talk to my dad about the way i see things he looked at me funny, then told me to shut up. it's getting harder though, because there seems to be more and more stuff i have to watch out for. that's what i call trip-trap.

trip-trap is all the things that i have to do to stop things going wrong, like not going the same way twice in a day. going twice somewhere in a day is only one example of evenshapehate. another example is that i don't like to use someone's name twice in the same day, so i make up other versions of their name in my head, so i can use those instead. that's evenshapehate for you. but evenshapehate is just one part of the trip-trap.

i can remember when there wasn't too much to worry about. it started with shoes. new shoes. and i think i decided i didn't like them. i didn't like them because they were new, which meant my old ones had worn out. i don't like it when things have to change.

but mum threw the old ones away, so i had to wear

the new shoes. what i did, to solve the problem, was make them old as quickly as i could. i scuffed them against walls as i went to school and walked through the thick mud at the edge of a couple of puddles.

it seemed to help.

but now i have to do it to all new things i get. i call it newchangeold. anything new i get i newchangeold, so when i got a new school bag i rolled it down a muddy slope, but three times, because once didn't seem to be enough, and i couldn't do it twice because of evenshapehate.

and that's the problem, everything's got so complicated, because of all the trip-trap, and because of how one bit of it might make another bit even more complicated.

there's dozens of things i have to be careful of now, things i have to do.

like at the end of every day i have to count up and work out if there's anything i've done an even number of times. if there is i have to do whatever it is one more time. even taking a leak.

sometimes it takes me for ever to go to bed.

and now i'm in more trouble, because my english teacher says i'm using bad language. she's been complaining about my writing. i'm not enjoying it, i can tell you that. it's just another example of getting into trouble for things that aren't my fault. my english teacher is a strange woman with crazy hair and an unorthodox way of doing things. but she's decided my approach to the english language is a bit too unorthodox.

the problem, as miss hess sees it, is that i've stopped using capital letters. stopped using them at the start of sentences, stopped using them for names, stopped using them for the first-person personal pronoun, by which i mean i.

miss mess had a go at me about this and asked what-the-intensifying-word i was playing at. so i gave her a long story about anarchism and the poet e e cummings and the ego of the pronoun, and she told me i was an intensifying-word moron. i was amazed a teacher could get away with using words like she uses in class, and i am not going to repeat them here. i don't like to hear bad words, it reminds me of home, too much.

anyway, miss dress basically told me to stop it or there would be qualifying-word trouble. i don't think she bought my story about the poet, the one i talked about, but to be honest that's fair, because that's not why i'm doing it. i don't like the way capitals are so important. just because they're the start of something new, they get a capital letter, and i don't like new things because, like i said, new things mean change. and change reminds me of the things going on at home.

things have been pretty difficult recently, that is true. the trip-trap has really been getting me down because of it getting so complicated. i was standing at the bus stop after school when i started thinking about the trip-trap. i was wondering whether i shouldn't be using the same word twice in the same sentence, just in case that was causing some of the bad things to happen to me. this is worrying me because it might very well be true, but i tried to resist accepting it as part of the rules, because it would get very hard to stick to it. it would be really hard, i mean, not to use a little word twice in one sentence. a word like to, or at, or the.

and although i might just get away with keeping an eye on that, i know what would happen next. what would happen next is that i'd have to extend it beyond each sentence to everything i said in five minutes. or an hour. or a day. and all the counting i'd have to do would drive me mad.

i don't want to think about it, because that would be impossible, and then i'd talk even less than i do now.

all this was going through my head as i got on the bus and made my way to somewhere nondescript to sit. not too near the front, not too near the back. those are the kind of places where trouble finds me. i sat in the row just in front of the one where the higher seats start, at the back. usually a safe seat.

i was about to get off at my stop, when i heard a voice behind me.

i shuddered because i could tell the voice was directed at me.

i looked round to see the girl who'd just moved to our school a couple of weeks ago. she's in my class in fact, but i hadn't ever spoken to her, and i didn't see why she had to speak to me, but something in what she said got my attention.

i used to do that, she said.

i thought her name was sandra, but I wasn't sure.

i didn't know what to say, and i said nothing. i opened my mouth though, which made me feel stupid, and then i started to panic. by the time i realised what was happening i had missed my stop.

i used to do that, she said, again. count the poles, she said.

then i really started to panic, because that's just what i had been doing. i had been counting the telegraph poles on the way home, and had to make sure i saw an odd number. to make sure, i counted the tens on my fingers, and did the units in my head.

i scrambled to my feet and got myself to the front of the bus, pushing every stop button as i went down.

the bus driver got cross with me and said that he wasn't going to stop any sooner for that even if i had missed my stop.

as i walked home, counting the extra poles i'd passed by missing my stop, i thought about the girl. sharon.

what crossed my mind first was to be shocked that she had spoken to me. what crossed my mind next was to wonder how she knew what i was doing. she might just have been able to see my fingers moving ever so slightly, racking up the tens, but that wouldn't mean anything to anyone. unless…

unless, she really had used to do it herself.

i saw her again the next day and she wouldn't leave me alone.

she came up to me first thing as soon as i got on the bus.

i'm sorry you missed your stop, she said.

she went on for a bit, and then she started on about counting things.

i started to freak out a bit inside, and looked around, but no one seemed to be listening. there was some scuffle going on at the back and most people were watching that.

she went on about counting things. i thought about getting cross with her to make her stop, but decided it would be better to ignore her, and hope she would give up. but she didn't.

i used to do that, she said, i had to make sure everything was in twos. you know? even.

and before i knew what i was saying i opened my mouth and spoke.

even? i said. no, it has to be odd.

and so then she knew that i knew what she was talking about, and i couldn't stop her.

she wasn't at school the next day, and she wasn't on the bus the following morning, but going home she was there again, and that's when i realised the thing. i realised that i liked her.

so when she said, do you want to have tea at my house one day? after school? i said i would.

great, she said. how about monday? i'm going to buy some new cds over the weekend, and we can listen to them.

i nodded.

what kind of music do you like? she asked.

music? i said.

she laughed.

yes, she said, music. what bands? metal? no, maybe not, maybe…skate? no? well, i give up, you tell me! but i couldn't, because i don't know.

there's no music in our house. my parents don't like it.

just tell me what the last cd you bought was, sarah said.

i looked at her, and opened my mouth and felt stupid, but said it anyway.

i've never bought a cd, i said. i don't have any music.

she looked back at me, but she wasn't smiling any more.

oh sweet intensifying-word, she said. a really intense word too.

so i'm going to her house on monday.

*

I really like Sarah, but not like I fancy her. She's funny and most of all she's good to talk to. About stuff, about anything. About music.

'Well, then,' she said, the first time I went to her house. 'If you don't know anything about music, I'm going to teach you.'

'Teach me?' I said. And I must have looked pretty shocked, because she laughed.

'Don't worry. All you have to do is tell me whether you like what I play you or not. Can you do that?'

'I think so,' I said, but I still felt pretty stupid.

So we've listened to hundreds of CDs since then. She has an enormous collection and her dad has even more because he used to work for a record company. To start with I found it really hard to even say whether I liked anything or not.

I would wait until something finished and just sit there. Once Sarah just burst out laughing.

'Don't look so serious!' she said. 'Just tell me what you think.'

I thought about leaving. I didn't like being laughed at. But I didn't want to upset her, so I stayed.

'Well,' she said.

She waited for an answer.

'I don't know,' I said. 'It was a bit…boring?'

'Good!' she said. 'I hate it too, I just thought I'd check you weren't deaf.'

And we both started to laugh.

Now I'm much better at it and I can just tell, immediately, whether I'm going to like it or not.

'Rubbish!' I shout, or maybe, 'Cool!'

And it's true. What happened on the bus, that time

we met, was true.

Sarah told me all about it. She said she used to count the poles too, but lots of other things too, to make sure everything was an even number. To make sure nothing bad happened. She counted so many things it got really difficult, and in the end she had to go and see a special doctor about it. She says she's much better now.

Better. Like she'd been ill.

That struck me. I didn't think I was ill.

So she was just like me, and says she still catches herself doing it sometimes. Counting. Just like me, except with me it's even numbers I don't like, with her it's odd.

That was what made me realise that it's all stupid.

And we talked about other stuff, about why I was writing like I was, and about names, and so on, and I felt so tired by it all that sometimes we would just sit and listen to music and not even say whether we liked it or not.

I felt tired, so tired. Listening to something really calm one day, I began to think about giving up the trip-trap. About letting it go. And I've begun not to worry about some of it so much.

I'm still not going to play any music at home, and besides, there's nothing to play it on, but Sarah lives

really close and she says I can go round any time.
I guess I first went to Sarah's house about a month
ago. Or maybe two. I don't know.

Because I haven't been counting.

8
Road Trip

by Kay Woodward

Road Trip

Thud, thud, thud, thud.

Her footsteps echoed miserably on the pavement. Jill gazed down at scuffed shoes as they dodged cracks and avoided potholes. Another day nearly over. And, for the sixty-third time that dreary day, she gave a hurricane-strength sigh. She'd made such a total mess of everything.

She glanced to the right. There they were – walking on the opposite pavement. Her ex-friends. Acting as if they were having the best time in the world. Whispering to each other. Giggling wickedly – their shoulders shivering with laughter. Jill knew that it was all for her benefit. They were showing her how together they were. And how alone she was.

'What are *you* looking at?' taunted Amber across the traffic.

Jill felt her cheeks prickle with heat as they both stared, hands planted firmly on hips. 'I don't know…the label's fallen off,' she said lamely.

Amber gave a short, sharp laugh and nudged Narinder. Abruptly, they walked on, sniggering and whispering as if their lives depended on it.

Jill trudged onwards. They'd fallen out before – the three of them – but they'd always made up straight afterwards. Things had never lasted *this* long.

If only she hadn't made that stupid *stupid* comment about Darren last week.

Darren was so dull he made Radio 4 sound riveting. Given the slightest encouragement, he would drone on about helicopters, aeroplanes or Formula One cars for hours. If it had an engine, Darren was hooked. He definitely had no time at all for girls.

At least, that was what Jill thought. So, when she, Amber and Narinder had been taking part in their favourite break-time activity of Picking The Perfect Boyfriend, that's exactly what Jill had said…

'Darren wouldn't recognise a girl if she was wearing a sandwich board saying *I'm a girl*,' she concluded.

'He's not that bad,' said Narinder. 'He was quite chatty at the Christmas disco.'

'That's only because he was explaining how aeroplane wings work,' Jill replied. 'Hmm. Aeronautical engineering versus make-up and music. No contest, is there?' She and Amber laughed loudly.

Narinder was silent.

'Oh, come on!' said Amber. 'You don't like him, do you?' She paused. 'Do you?'

'Well…er…'

'But he's got freckles…' said Jill incredulously. Then she added the final insult. 'And he's ginger!'

'He's *auburn*!' Narinder bellowed. Dramatically, she

burst into tears and ran off towards the toilets.

'Now look what you've done!' said Amber crossly. 'You and your motor mouth!' She hurried after Narinder.

For a second or two, Jill was lost for words. Then, as if she'd had a bucket of icy water thrown at her, she jolted into action. Speeding after her two best friends in the whole world, she gave herself a quick telling off for being so thoughtless. OK, so Darren wasn't her cup of chai, but there was no reason why he shouldn't be Narinder's. And if he promised not to bore her with the workings of the jet engine, she might even be able to put up with his company. She caught up with Narinder and began her apology.

Thud, thud, thud, thud.

Jill's feet pounded on and on… past the Boots where they used to search for the newest, blackest mascara…past the newsagents where they once flicked through the latest, glossiest mags. She sneaked a look across the road. There they were. Still busy leaving her out in the cold.

Without warning, Narinder caught her eye. Jill stared back, warily. Did this mean that the ice queens were defrosting?

Neeeeeowww!

A motorbike roared past and the spell was broken. Narinder's eyes hardened, she nudged Amber and the two of them glared at Jill.

'What's *your* problem?' jeered Amber. 'Run out of friends, have you? No one left to insult?'

'Listen,' said Jill, struggling to be heard over the traffic. 'There's been one misunderstanding after another. I never meant to hurt anyone—'

'Can you hear anything?' Amber said loudly to Narinder, who shook her head in reply.

'Just an awful whining noise.'

'Thought so.' Amber flicked long hair over her shoulder. 'Ooooh, look at the time! Come on! We don't want to be late for *you know what.*'

'Cool!' said Narinder at top volume.

Jill grimaced. OK, she'd got the message. There was to be no truce.

After she'd said sorry to Narinder for being insensitive and rude – and gingerist and frecklist – things had got back to normal. Almost. The three of them had still hung out together. They had still spent hours in Boots and made their thumbs ache with too much texting. But something wasn't quite right. Narinder wasn't quite as friendly as before, no matter how much she denied it. And she and Amber began spending more and more time together – just the two of them.

It wasn't much fun being left out.

Then, Jill had put her foot in it again – big style.

It happened during one wet break, the three of them slumped at their desks, raindrops hammering against the classroom windows…

Narinder picked absent-mindedly at a loose thread on her tie. 'I can't wait till I'm fourteen,' she said.

'Me neither,' said Jill, tilting her chair back at a dangerous angle. 'But my birthday's not for months.'

'I wonder what sort of party I'll have?' mused Narinder. 'Fancy dress? A 1980s party? I suppose I'm far too old for pass the parcel…'

Jill spluttered, waving her hands wildly, 'Of *course* you're too old. Besides, don't you think birthday parties are a bit – well – young? A bit *passé*? A bit *last year*?'

Narinder nodded slowly. 'Suppose so.'

Amber was resting her chin on her hands, gazing at the whiteboard.

'Don't you agree?' Jill asked, her chair legs clanging back on to the floor.

'Hmm?' said Amber, looking puzzled. 'But didn't you have a p—'

The jangling bell drowned out her next words and, by home time, Jill had totally forgotten the discussion.

The following morning, Jill remembered her own words in exact, cringeworthy detail. Because, by the following morning, every other girl in her class had been invited to Amber's Thirteenth Birthday Sleepover. Every girl except Jill.

'I'm so sorry,' Jill said to Amber at break time. She was beginning to feel that all she ever did was apologise and grovel. It was perfect training for a career in a complaints department, but about as much fun as eating Marmite. 'I totally forgot that your thirteenth birthday was coming up,' she added. 'I meant that *fourteenth* birthday parties were a bit naff, not thirteenth. I meant—'

'I know exactly what you meant,' said Amber. 'And that's why you're not coming. After all, you're far too grown-up to be invited to something so *young* and so *last year.*'

'But—'

Amber continued as if Jill hadn't spoken. 'Now you'll have the evening free to read the telephone directory or learn Swahili or crochet a duvet cover – or whatever.' She looked at her watch. 'Must dash – lots of childish, immature birthday things to do—'

'But...'

No amount of butting was going to put it right. Amber had gone – sweeping Narinder away with her.

Jill shivered. There was a definite chill in the air.

*

Thud, thud, thud, thud.

She reached the park. Jill looked between the railings at the empty swings swaying gently to and fro in the breeze. A cluster of girls lounged against the climbing frame, gossiping lazily. She stared at them – envious of their friendly chatter. Then she swivelled her head and stared at *them*. Two best mates walking home from school together – on the other side of the road. They might as well be on the other side of the world.

Today was Amber's birthday. And, ever since infants' school, they'd always made a big deal of birthdays. They swapped presents wrapped in spangly paper, festooned with ribbons and coated with glitter. (The wrapping was usually more impressive than the present.) They squeezed in quick verses of *Happy Birthday* between lessons. Birthdays were so cool.

This one was frosty.

Even so, Jill had bought a present as usual. The situation might be desperate, they might never ever be friends again, but she still felt a nudge of loyalty. So, before pupils had flooded the school corridors that morning, Jill had tucked a perfectly wrapped box into her ex-friend's locker. Nestling inside were pink sparkly hair slides. Amber would know who they were from.

Bored.

Jill was bored of all the huffing and puffing and whining and whingeing and name-calling and bickering. OK, so if there were an Olympic event for Putting Your Foot In It, she'd have won the gold… An unexpected smile crept on to her lips at the thought. Glancing right, Jill caught Amber's eye. Too late, she realised that she was grinning right at her.

Unexpectedly, a smile flashed across Amber's face. But, just as quickly, she turned away, her shiny hair swinging round as if she were rehearsing for a shampoo ad. And there, in her hair, was something pink and sparkly.

Jill felt a flicker of hope. Amber was wearing her birthday present! Did this mean that everything was going to be OK?

Then, Narinder looked in her direction, her lip curling upwards – not into a smile, but into a sneer.

The flicker of hope was promptly snuffed out.

Once Jill had made the birthday blunder, Narinder had rushed to Amber's defence. The two of them were closer than the bumpers of gridlocked cars.

And, when the rumours began, Jill knew exactly who the culprit was.

Last year, when she'd been much younger and much more foolish, Jill had suffered a brief crush on Mr Pearson, the history teacher. Tall, willowy, dark and brooding, he'd looked fresh from the set of a TV costume drama. It hadn't taken many weeks – OK, months – for Jill to realise that the teacher was far too old for her. He was at least thirty. And he had wrinkles.

Jill had trusted Narinder with this classified information and Narinder had sworn never to breathe a word of it.

Now that battle lines had been drawn, Narinder appeared to have breathed the secret to the whole of Year Eight. But she'd neglected to mention to Year Eight that Jill had crushed the crush long ago.

Rhymes and ridicule, jeers and gibing – that's all she'd heard for the last couple of days. Whenever it happened, Jill clamped her lips tightly shut, fixing them into her best sarcastic smile. If she answered back, they'd never leave her alone. If she ignored it, they'd get bored – eventually. She kept schtum, even when Darren the Dullard joined in, hoping to impress Narinder with his boy-band singing ability.

Jill and Pearson up a tree
K. I. K. I.
Jill and Pearson up a tree
K. I. S. S. I. N. G.

Jill couldn't help feeling hurt. Where her clumsy comments had been accidental, Narinder's had been deliberate. She was sick of being attacked – it was time to take action.

So, earlier that day, she had cornered Narinder after double Maths…

'Got any more out-of-date secrets up your sleeve?' Jill said.

Narinder had the decency to go pink. 'I…er…'

'You could always start making stuff up,' continued Jill, warming to her topic. 'Why stop at secrets you said you'd take to the grave – secrets you said no one would be able to drag out of you, not if they were dangling you by your big toe over a barrel of boiling oil? Why not make up some brand-new *lies* about me instead?'

'I didn't mean to tell anyone,' Narinder spluttered. 'It just slipped out and then one of the boys heard and then…and then…everyone knew.'

'Yeah, right,' said Jill.

'At least I don't go around making nasty comments about people's boyfriends!' muttered Narinder.

'I didn't!'

'You did. And you ruin people's birthday parties.'

'I do not!'

'Do so!'

This was getting silly – so silly that Jill felt an unexpected giggling bubbling up inside her. Making sure that her face was straighter than a BBC newsreader's, she carried on.

'Do not! *You* made me look a pillock!'

'You *are* a pillock!'

'*You're* a divvy!'

'And you're *both* inside when you should be enjoying the sunshine,' said Mrs Spinks, the English teacher. 'Think of all that lovely vitamin D going to waste. Out – *now!*'

Thud, thud, thud, thud.

Jill walked on, past the bus stop, past the zebra crossing, keeping pace with Amber and Narinder. The river of cars and buses flowed between – dividing them, yet somehow holding them together. One thing was certain. Breaking friends might be tough, but making friends again was even tougher.

She chewed on the skin at the side of her thumb, wondering what they were talking about. Wondering who would make the first move. What if no one did? What if Amber and Narinder never wanted to be friends again? What if she was shunned for the rest of her school days? Surely she was too young to be a social outcast? Wasn't she?

Jill was tired of asking herself questions that she couldn't answer. She just wanted her friends back.

A faint chanting sound floated above the noise of the cars that streamed past.

Jill and Pearson up a tree

Not again.

K. I. K. I.

Jill gritted her teeth.

Jill and Pearson up a tree

Her bottom jaw jutted out further and further.

K. I. S. S. I. N. G.

She took a great gulp of air and then spun round to face her tormentors. Despite her decision to be grown-up and aloof, words flew out of her mouth. 'Why don't you just grow up!' she roared.

'Ooooooooooh,' said Darren, grinning widely. 'I'm really, like, scared.'

'You will be, if you don't leave me alone,' warned Jill, feeling about as threatening as a knight with a rubber sword.

'You want to be careful what you say,' said one of the bigger lads. He moved forwards.

Jill moved backwards.

'Yeah,' said another, from over her shoulder. 'Not exactly Miss Popular at the moment, are you? I don't see anyone rushing to your defence.'

Thud-thud, thud-thud. It was her heart that was pounding now.

'If you want to know,' Jill began, sounding braver than she felt, 'I have plenty of friends.'

'Then where are they?' said Darren, raising his eyebrows questioningly.

'Here,' said Narinder.

'You what?' said Darren, confused.

'You heard,' said Narinder. She and Amber leapt from the black and white crossing on to the pavement. Behind them, traffic surged once more.

'Hey, we were only having a laugh,' said Darren. 'Anyway, it was *you* that told us she fancied Mr Pearson.'

Statue-like, Jill looked at Narinder.

'Well, I was wrong,' said her ex-friend.

Her friend.

'Leave her alone,' added Amber, for good measure.

Jill grinned.

'Girls,' muttered Darren. His mates mumbled in agreement. One by one, they all began to slink away.

The three girls looked at each other.

'So, what are you wearing tonight?' Amber asked, linking an arm through Jill's.

'Me? Tonight?' said Jill. She didn't understand. Surely they weren't making up, were they? *Were they?*

'To the sleepover?' said Narinder, linking her other arm.

'Well,' said Jill. A grin began to twitch at the corner of her mouth. 'I thought I'd go for…pyjamas.'

They were friends again.

For today, at least.

9

The Wrong Party

by Helen Oyeyemi

The Wrong Party

Sade hung over the back of her sister's chair, her hands buried in the long, soft swathes of purple gauze that was thrown over it. She watched Doyin's reflection in the mirror. Her sister was carefully applying eyeliner with a steady hand, drawing kohl in little swirls on her skin so that she looked almost like an Egyptian princess. Her purple streaked braids, styled into a sharp, straight bob, skimmed her bare brown shoulders.

'Do I look OK?' Doyin asked, finally, wrinkling her nose at Sade in the mirror when she'd finished. Her hands fluttered nervously over her throat, where her purple halterneck top was loosely knotted.

It was Valentine's night; the night before Sade's thirteenth birthday, and Doyin was going out to dinner with her boyfriend, Toby, even though their parents disapproved of him. Toby was white, and two years older than Doyin, who was seventeen. Before Sade could answer, Doyin started spraying perfume on her wrists and behind her ears, sniffing daintily at the air with a smile.

'You're flipping gorgeous, as usual,' Sade told Doyin's reflection, trying not to sound jealous. It wasn't fair that she looked so different from her sister – no matter how many times Doyin told her that she used to get confronted on the bus and told she was ugly, too, it was hard to take. It was hard to swallow back the tears that drummed like a rainfall at the back of her head whenever it happened.

'Someone at school said you were weird today,' Sade said, after a little while, feeling mean even as she tried to pay her sister back for being pretty. Doyin didn't immediately reply, but gave a shrug. As Sade's eyes skimmed over her, she noted Doyin's slightly protruding collarbones, noticed that Doyin still hadn't quite put on all the weight that she'd lost before, in the bad times, when she'd still been at Sade's school. This was why people at school thought she was weird. For a long time, Doyin had hardly eaten anything, but she had pretended that she ate lots. Her eyes had suddenly seemed far too big for her face. She would reel off sentences that didn't fit together, then put her hands over her face as if catching herself so that she wouldn't fall, dizzy, to the ground. And whenever she smiled during that time, it was as if the corners of her mouth had been dragged up with pins that dug into her flesh. But even now, when she was much better and eating again, if you said the words 'eating disorder' to Doyin, her lips pressed tight and thin and she would stare away until you stopped talking about it.

Sade, who loved her sister more than anyone or anything else in the world, had jumped on Tom Wilson, the boy who'd sneered that Doyin was weird, and punched him until she was dragged off by her friend Kelly and pulled out of sight of the teacher on playground duty. He didn't tell on her, even though she'd split his lip, because he didn't want anyone to know that a girl had beaten him up.

'Football hit me in the face, Miss,' he'd said, at registration, bowing his tousled brown head and staring at his desk as a few others, who had seen what happened, snickered at the back of the class.

'So it's your birthday tomorrow – are you excited?' Sade heard Doyin saying, as she got up and moved round the room to rummage in her black and silver purse for her mobile phone. Sade turned to peer at her; Doyin's eyes looked huge again, but it was only the eyeliner.

'What's to be excited about? My birthday happens every year,' Sade said slowly, looking quickly at her sister to see if she looked about to reveal a plan. For Sade's twelfth birthday, Doyin had crowned her Queen Titania and held a small party for her and her best friends in the garden. Stretched out on pale pink and blue rugs they'd eaten multi-coloured flower petals made of brittle spun sugar, and listened to music, and

147

blown bubbles so that they danced away on the air with rainbows glinting all over them. For Sade's eleventh birthday party, her friends had to help her hunt for little presents, which were hidden in various places, both at school and at home – in the house and garden. In the evening they had told ghost stories in a tent set up in the living room.

Doyin, on the floor now, wriggled out from under the bed and waved her mobile phone in the air triumphantly, before climbing to her feet, smoothing out her skirt, and beginning to dial. 'I don't think I'll be helping you celebrate your thirteenth, Sade,' she said, not looking at Sade but at the wall as she listened to the phone ringing on the other end. 'I'm not trying to be funny, but I think thirteen's a horrible age to be – it's nothing to celebrate; I wouldn't go back to being thirteen for the world.'

Sade started to protest, then shrugged unhappily and wandered away as Toby answered and Doyin flopped down onto her messy bed and started talking to him in a low, sweet voice. Sade supposed she could understand; the whole weird eating thing had started for Doyin when she was thirteen. But Doyin's wacky plans had made Sade's birthdays happy. So their parents would make special food and give her cards and presents, it wouldn't be the same without some

Doyin-devised entertainment for her and her friends. She checked the time – it was only seven o'clock, which meant that her mum had only just started her night shift at the hospital, and her dad would still be napping before dinner at eight. Sade decided to run down to the park and see who was there.

'I'm going to the park,' she shouted up the stairs, snatching her coat and jamming her feet into her trainers. Nobody answered, so she left noisily, banging the door behind her.

Tom Wilson and his eleven-year-old brother, Mark, were there, whooping like sirens as they took turns jumping crazily onto the roundabout in the fading daylight, whirling until they were just a blur of faces. As soon as Sade saw them she rolled her eyes and began to walk past, over to the other side of the park, where there were benches by the swings. Tom, who was thirteen already, was always making horrible comments to and about her, comments which she usually managed to ignore, except for earlier that day.

When Tom saw her he leapt off the roundabout, which was creaking to a halt, and sped towards her, letting out a savage, ululating cry. Startled, she began to back away. He laughed and stopped a few feet from her. He was still wearing his school uniform, but he'd slicked his hair up into a glossy brown peak, probably with water, and his school shirt was falling out from under his blue pullover. He had streaky mud and grass stains on the bottoms of his trousers.

'Scared now, are you?' he jeered, narrowing his eyes and folding his arms.

'No,' Sade shot back, balling her hands up into fists. Mark eagerly jumped off the roundabout too and started running around her in circles, stamping rings around her so that she couldn't follow him without her eyes crossing. Tom joined in, dancing around her making more strange, hollow noises and, frightened now, Sade waited for a heartbeat's length with her eyes fixed on the swings, then broke through their ring and made for the benches, her breath scratching hoarsely out of her. She knew a way, through the bushes behind the benches and over the back gate of the park, that she could get back home without them being able to follow her. The park gate was high, and she didn't know a single other person who dared climb it, who trusted themselves to drop, clumsily, hard, but safely, on the ground at the bottom.

Tom caught her as she fought through the dense, fuzzy green of the bushes, catching her around the waist and twisting her around roughly so she was forced to face him. He grabbed her by the wrists before she could make a swing for him, laughing as she tried to bite him. He wore a moustache of sweat on his top lip, and his hair peak was collapsing. When she screamed, he let her go suddenly, and she stumbled, then fell heavily, her long, denim-clad legs sprawling out on the ground, before beginning to struggle to her feet again. He strode over to her and held her down, planting his hands on her shoulders as he bent to peer into her face, a worried wrinkle of skin appearing between his dark brown eyes. She struggled even more fiercely, wondering if she could head-butt him.

'Look, I'm sorry for calling your sister weird, OK?' he said, abruptly, and in the dusk she could see how fine and light his eyelashes were, and how dark his eyes were through the wavy strands of hair that had fallen over his forehead. His arms were skinny, but strong, forcing her to hold still. In the distance, they could both hear strident voices and the rusty *wheeeeeeee* of the roundabout, and they knew that Mark had found some other friend.

'You don't even know her – you only say she's weird because you hear other people say that,' Sade said fiercely, starting off loud and fast, but weakening on the last words, her voice growing slower, as Tom leaned closer to her, tilting his head with a soft, puzzled expression before he kissed her slightly open mouth with warm lips.

'Um...happy Valentine's Day,' he said, hesitantly.

Sade noted, distantly, that he smelt of sweat and salt and vinegar crisps, before she struggled out of his slack grasp and ran for the gate, scrambling up it, her sure hands gripping and clinging to it as she hauled herself onwards. He called her, and she ignored him, panting as she reached the top of the gate, swung a leg over it and began down the other side. She caught sight of his face as he stood amongst the bushes, a life-sized schoolboy doll (silent now, and staring)...

something

made

her

lose

her

footing.

She fell awkwardly, swinging at first from one arm as she skimmed the ground, then hit it hard, biting the inside of her cheek as she did so. She felt something small and frail, seeping out red pain, skittering around inside her skull, and then she realised that Tom was shouting out from the other side of the gate, and that she couldn't move. She was spiked all over with hurting arrows that fixed her to the ground as if she were growing out of it. To move would be to die. She had never had such a bad headache; someone had to stop that ball from rolling around inside her head...

She managed to turn her gaze upwards. A woman, a kind-faced, familiar, white woman in a brown coat bent over her, lips pursed in consternation as she said: 'Are you all right? What's the matter? Can you get up? Try and get up,' over and over. Sade smiled; it was like watching television – she was no part of this.

'Mummy...Doyin,' she said, laughing now, even though it hurt to let the air come out. 'I hurt...I hurt my head.'

And then she fell asleep.

When Sade woke up, she was in a bare, white, high-ceilinged room that she did not know. The windows were set in frames like arches. Sunlight beaded on her eyelashes, and as she stirred, she was surprised to find that she lay on a low, fluffy white mattress heaped with piles and piles of patchwork quilts. At first, she couldn't move for all the quilting, but then she managed to twist her body and roll out from under them. She was still wearing her jeans and baggy blue jumper. She knelt by the mattress and inspected the different patches on the quilts, puzzled. Each patch had a different face stitched into it; girls and boys, some faces half-familiar with different coloured cross-stitched eyes and open-mouthed smiles in smooth lines of thread.

She fleetingly touched her lips, her cheek, and thought, half-frowning, half-smiling, of Tom.

She thought that it must be morning, and therefore her thirteenth birthday.

At about the same time she noticed the absolute silence. She couldn't hear cars or trees. She couldn't hear anything, not even a cough. Drowsily wondering where she was, and where everybody had gone, Sade stood and tried to look out of the window, but the sunlight covered the glass panes like a dazzling golden curtain, and she couldn't see past it. There was nothing but harsh light outside. Feeling a tugging constriction around her wrist as she tried to sit back down again, she glanced at it distractedly, expecting to see a wristband of some kind. Instead, she saw that there was a wide loop of crimson ribbon tied around her wrist, the rest of its length trailing off out of the door of the room in a glowing stream.

As she followed the ribbon to the door with her eye and felt the weight of the silence everywhere, she had to stifle a heart-slamming shriek as she felt a small but strong tug on her wrist again. *I'm not scared, no I'm not.*

Trembling, she got up and began to pace the ribbon's length, following it out of the room and down a long, white corridor that had rows and rows of other, closed, doors set into its walls. The corridor was so bright that she had to narrow her eyes as she followed the trail of ribbon leading from her wrist. Her feet were bare and felt cold and numb, even though the floors were so thickly carpeted that her footsteps made no sound. She began to feel exhausted, as if she had been walking down the corridor for hours and hours, even though she was sure that she had only just started.

Once, tiring of following the ribbon's tug, Sade pushed rebelliously at the handle of one of the many doors, wondering what was behind it and if there were anyone or anything there that might give her a clue where she was. She stood outside and looked into the room, which was windowless and painted dull yellow. The room was filled with nothing but air and silence.

Then she noticed the long, sloping shadow that sliced across the ceiling of the room; the shadow of a tall man in a top hat, his head bent so that it was almost as if he were looking at her.

She gasped, and skipped back, scanning the room before her, then looking behind her, then up and down the endless white cube of the corridor.

No one was there; how could there be a shadow?

When she gazed back up at the ceiling of the yellow room, the shadow was gone. Then she saw it; looming darkly on the floor, a sticky stain creeping. Creeping, hands outstretched. It took all her strength not to scream; it took all her strength to slam the door shut as quickly as she could.

I'm thirteen now; I'm more than a child, I will be OK.

Her lips were pressed tight, stretched over her teeth, and she tried to think of nothing at all as she continued down the corridor, steadfastly ignoring all the other doors.

Finally, when she had a whole mass of ribbon tangled into a fat loop behind her, she reached the end of the red ribbon trail, a half-open door set into the end wall of the corridor. Through the gap, between the door and the wall she could see sections of the room; multicoloured balloons floating, parts of a table laid out for a party with streamers strewn all over it. She rocked on the balls of her feet, confused; had Doyin arranged something after all?

She pushed open the door. There was a huge banner spanning the room: *'Happy 13th, Sade!'* and fragments of green and pink streamers floated through the air. An enormous tower of a cake sat in the centre of a long table. There were lots and lots of people sitting around the table, wearing silver-striped party hats, plates full of sweets and crisps set in front of them. Doyin was there and so was Tom, further down the end of the table, and Sade's parents were there too, and her best friends, Carrie and Kelly. Carrie had her dark red hair done up in shiny, swishing pigtails with green ribbon, and Kelly had her face painted to look like a zebra. Lots of the people at the table were people Sade didn't really know; there was a small, round, old lady that she had never seen in her life.

The table was full of people; the room was full of people, but as Sade stood, tired and dazed, surrounded by rivers of red ribbon, on the threshold of her birthday party, no one jumped up and shouted:

'SURPRISE!'

No one even moved, or spoke, or even seemed to breathe.

'I'm dreaming,' Sade whispered, knowing that she didn't dare to step into that room. 'It's all a horrible dream. Or something has happened,' she said, a little louder.

No one stirred, or moved to answer her.

'I've got to go back to sleep!' she said, shrilly, trying to untangle the ribbon. If you went to sleep in a dream, did that mean you would be able to wake up in the real world?

Giving up on the knotted red material, she began to run, almost flying, down the corridor, looking for her room, looking for the only open door, the room where the mattress and the light and the patchwork quilts were.

She soon discovered, her feet pounding against the carpet as she ran from one end of the corridor to the other, that she couldn't find it any more; all the doors were closed. She began to cry, wet salt pouring down her face as she remembered that she didn't dare to open a closed door.

She didn't know what else to do, so somehow she managed to tear the ribbon from her wrist, sitting down with her back against the wall and working at it with her teeth until it fell silently away from her.

Then... 'Don't cry, Sade,' a girl said, opening the door opposite.

She stood, framed in darkness, her long, thin, black braids pouring over her shoulders. Her eyes were red from weeping, and she blinked them slowly as Sade scrambled up and clutched the wall, gaping. The girl was familiar; Sade recognised her from somewhere else, long ago – she recognised the enormous eyes, the flaking skin on the girl's lips, her tired, gaunt stoop –

'Doyin?'

Doyin didn't reply to her, but stood aside in the doorway, and beckoned.

'You went to the wrong party, before,' she whispered. 'I've done that too, but it's all right now. Hurry.'

Fearing a trick, but also fearing to be left alone again, Sade stood and took Doyin's outstretched hand. This party was bright and loud and full of colours and people kissing her, hugging her, sweeping her up. Someone she knew, but she was never quite sure exactly who, said: 'Thirteen years without falling off the face of the earth! Well done!' and the person laughed, and laughed, until they were just a swirl in the back of her mind, scrunched up into the ball of her pain as she opened her eyes wide and looked at the brown coat woman who had bent over her in the park.

'Are you all right?' the woman said again, her face swimming in and out of focus beside Tom's concerned one.

Sade spat out a tooth and sat up tentatively, feeling bruised.

'Yeah,' she said. 'It's my birthday tomorrow.'

10
The Anorak's First Kiss

by John McLay

The Anorak's First Kiss

'Are you sure you want to see this?'

'Definitely. Are you sure you want me to see it?'

Jack hesitated, his fingers shaking slightly as he laid his palm against his bedroom door. Was he sure? He smiled, but he couldn't stop his stomach lurching south towards his slightly wobbly legs. He was, without a doubt, very, very nervous. Here was a girl – a really pretty one, too – who was in his home, who seemed sane and who wanted to see what his bedroom looked like.

This did not happen every day.

This had never actually happened to Jack before. 'Of course I want you to. I need you to see it.'

Behind him, Lucy grinned. She was so beautiful. She was wearing a white T-shirt and blue jeans and she had no make-up on – she didn't need it. 'OK, Jack, well lead the way then,' she said. 'Your Mam's got the food in the oven downstairs and it'll be ready soon. We can't wait here on the landing all day.'

'OK.' Jack breathed in and then pushed the door hard enough for it to swing open almost all the way. Lucy stepped past him and went inside. Jack crossed his fingers, screwed his eyes shut and muttered to himself under his breath as he followed her in. 'Please don't let her think I'm a total freak.' He was thirteen now, not eight. Shouldn't he have left all his obsessions from childhood behind by now? What was she going to think?

Jack's new friend from school, Lucy Hepburn, who, amazingly, and against all of his previous life history and experience, happened to be a girl, had stopped a few feet inside the room. She was now turning her head slowly from side to side, and then looking up and then down. They were the unmistakable actions of a person trying to take in the enormity of the sight in front of her.

Jack thought he heard her inhale sharply. But maybe he imagined that. She made a kind of popping sound with her mouth. What did that mean? Was it good or bad? He tried to follow her gaze from the direction her head was pointing in. What was she thinking? Was that just a perceptible step backwards towards the exit – towards escape from the nutter's bedroom she had just crazily agreed to enter? He hoped not.

He'd found it so hard to make friends recently. They all seemed to be into different things from him – clothes, sport and just…messing about really. These were things they thought of as cool. Jack liked all of these things too, but just not to the same degree. He made room in his life for something else altogether – and Lucy had just found out what it was.

Jack exhaled loudly. He'd been holding his breath for what seemed like ages. 'Well?' he said, tentatively. 'What do you think? Am I certifiable or what?'

Lucy turned round to look at him and, remarkably, was not wearing a horrified-face look. It was more a girl-in-awe face look. 'It's incredible,' she said. 'You really like *Doctor Who*, don't you?'

'Just a bit, yes.'

'I mean, you so totally, completely, really, really dig it. It's your thing. Your passion. You wake up to it, you go to bed to it. You eat it, you sleep it.'

Jack nodded. 'Pretty much so.' He looked around at his poster-covered walls and shelves laden with memorabilia. It was a shrine to his favourite television programme and he was definitely one of its most frequent and dedicated worshippers. He couldn't deny it. Even now, he smiled automatically when he looked at his life-size cardboard promotional cut-out, beside his desk, of Tom Baker dressed as the Fourth Doctor. He nodded knowingly when his eyes rolled appreciatively over a poster on the wall of Leela, one of the sexier female *Doctor Who* companions. He had a framed photograph on his bedside table, reminding him daily of the night not so long ago when he had met Christopher Ecclestone, after he'd appeared in a play at his local theatre. Might he, Jack Dawson, really have been the first person ever to get the autograph of the Ninth Doctor after the official press release announcing his appointment?

Lucy moved towards his bookshelf, almost floor to ceiling in size, and ran a finger along Jack's collection of associated books connected with the cult programme. Many were shrink-wrapped, or bagged protectively in transparent wallets.

'Can I open the curtains?' said Lucy. 'I can't see everything clearly.'

'I'll do it,' said Jack. He pulled back the curtains and tucked them neatly behind the sofa in front of the window. 'It's late enough for there not to be too much sun anymore. It fades the spines, you see.' Jack cringed when he realised how that must have sounded. What an anorak.

Lucy nodded but she clearly wasn't listening. She was too busy taking it all in. Probably too busy trying to get her head round what she had let herself in for.

Lucy was different from other girls and Jack couldn't help really liking her. She seemed more in control of her life, somehow. From their previous conversations at school break times, and in class, he knew that Lucy had moved around a lot because of her dad's work and that she had been to loads of different schools. She'd met a lot of different people in her life already so maybe that's what had helped give her so much confidence. Jack was only ever on solid ground about things he knew really well – like *Doctor Who*.

'Do you want to sit down?' said Jack. 'I can understand if you're a bit freaked out.'

Lucy picked up a disc from a neat stack beside Jack's all-in-one bedside TV and DVD player. She studied the front cover for a moment. '*The Seeds of Death*.' She picked up another couple. '*Earthshock. Vengeance on Varos*.'

She looked at Jack. 'Do you have them all on DVD, then?'

Was that a hint of sarcasm in her voice? Or was she really just interested? Jack's insides flipped over again. He sat down on the sofa and crossed his legs underneath him. 'Er, no. They're still mostly on video at the moment. Look in the wardrobe.'

Lucy raised an eyebrow with a smile. 'The wardrobe? Are you sure you want me to see your underwear so early in our relationship, Jack?'

Relationship? Were they having a relationship already? That had thrown him.

Lucy opened the wardrobe doors. Inside, the shelves were laden with BBC VHS videotapes. Their almost uniform black spines en masse created an impressive sight. 'Blimey. I never knew there were so many different epidodes.'

'There's hundreds. It's being going since 1963

remember,' said Jack. 'But why would you know. You're a girl – you're probably not into cult science-fiction series.'

Damn. Why had he said that?

'Hey, don't jump to conclusions, matey,' said Lucy. 'I know a bit. I remember seeing the Daleks and the Cybermen when I was young. My dad's into stuff like this too – I've seen some stories when he's been watching it. He's more of a Trekkie but I know he has a few Doctor Who bits. The odd DVD, I think.'

Jack looked down and stared at his feet, sheepishly. 'Really? Sorry! I didn't mean that. About not liking this stuff because you're a girl. I'm not sure why I said it. I'm a bit nervous.'

Why *had* he said that? He was just so desperate to keep the conversation going he was gabbling. Now he was getting the distinct feeling that this was not going as well as it might have. In all their previous conversations at school he hadn't mentioned his leaning towards the wandering Time Lord and his adventures in space. So far they'd just talked about normal stuff, like homework and friends and films and food. They'd laughed so much and he hadn't tripped over his words once in all that time. By not mentioning this big thing in his life had he ruined everything? Had he misled her into thinking he was something he clearly was not?

'No worries,' said Lucy. 'I forgive you.'

Jack breathed a sigh of relief. Lucy smiled and Jack suddenly wanted to jump up and kiss her.

NO!

What was he thinking?

What an idiot. Slow down. It's going OK. She's still here. She hadn't left, laughing hysterically in his face and shouting, 'Wait till the kids at school hear about you, you bloody weirdo.' She was here, in his bedroom. Looking through his stuff, chatting. It was normal. This was what friends did all the time. But a snog was definitely not on the cards.

'So how long have you been into *Doctor Who*?' said Lucy. She came and sat next to him on the sofa. They weren't actually touching, but her weight on the spongy cushions made him lean slightly towards her.

Jack shifted his bodyweight slightly to compensate and inched away nervously. He hoped she hadn't noticed. 'Since I was eight. I started watching it on UK Gold and just got hooked.'

Lucy nodded. 'So you've collected this little lot in five years? Have you spent all the money on it that you've ever had, like, ever?'

'Almost everything. Birthday gifts, my paper-round wages.' Jack saw that Lucy was about to ask about his job so he just carried on straight away. 'I do a paper round seven days a week and help out a bloke I know who runs a merchandise stall at *Doctor Who* conventions. He pays me part cash, part collectibles. I get great deals from him.'

'You go to conventions? Blimey.'

Yikes. Should he have admitted to so much? Oh well, it was done now, might as well tell her the rest.

'And I trade a bit on Ebay,' he said. 'I've made quite a lot of money buying stuff cheap and then re-selling it.'

Jack couldn't tell if he'd impressed the girl sitting in his bedroom – yes, the *girl* sitting in *his* bedroom – or exposed another unnecessary layer to his alleged freakiness. Damn. Why did he keep going on about it all? He watched her look around the room some more and then turn towards him. 'So. Shall we have a snog, then?'

Eh?

Suddenly, it was Jack's turn for sharp intake of breath. He closed his eyes and then opened them again quickly.

Yup. She was still there.

'Er, did you just say what I thought you said.'

Please say yes. Please say yes.

Lucy smiled again and edged towards him a bit. 'Yes. I'd like a snog now please. You're cute and I like you. And I'm really turned on by Cybermen.'

Jack gulped. Had he died and gone to Gallifrey?

'OK, then.' Not knowing what else to do, and never having kissed a girl ever before, he closed his eyes and leaned forward towards her.

STOP!

'Stop!' he said. He opened his eyes and sat back. 'Hang on a minute.'

Lucy opened her eyes and sat back too.

'What? Don't you want to?'

'Yes,' said Jack. 'Yes of course I bloody want to. I so do. It's just that…you really don't mind?'

'Mind what?' she said, in a matter-of-fact voice.

'This. All of this?' He gestured wildly around him. 'My crazy *Doctor Who* thing that I've got going on. It's a bit of a bombshell isn't it? Doesn't it *bother* you?'

'No. Not at all. Sure, it's kinda weird to think you wear TARDIS slippers and have no clothes in your wardrobe – but I can live with that. Now come here.'

Then she touched Jack's shoulder gently and moved back towards him, angling her head slightly.

Jack had no qualms about locking on this time. He shot a quick positional glance at Lucy's approaching, fantastically beautiful face and then closed his eyes.

'Oh. OK, then,' he just managed to slip out before contact.

Their lips touched.

Jack trembled and felt an incredible electricity shoot

through him and spread directly outwards from their point of contact. He smelt her nice smell as he moved his lips in sync with hers. It was delicate and considered.

It wasn't a sloppy kiss. It felt so natural. He held back his tongue for as long as he could, but suddenly found that Lucy's own tongue was probing his mouth a little. Their tongues touched and he trembled again.

It still wasn't sloppy. Somehow their lips, still locked together, felt totally right together.

Jack instinctively moved his hand so that it rested on her knee. It felt the right thing to do. It wasn't too forward, but it was somehow intimate.

She squeezed his shoulder, and rubbed it a bit.

Jack lost himself to her for a few minutes. Later on he would not be able to remember how long they were actually in this position. Kissing!

He couldn't believe he was doing this. He'd dreamt about this moment for months, ever since she'd first said hello to him on her first day at his school in their Geography class.

At the same time, they moved apart.

Jack was grinning from ear to ear.

Lucy was smiling coyly and her cheeks had a little colour all of a sudden.

'I enjoyed that,' said Jack.

Damn. Why did he say that? How uncool.

'Sorry.' Jack stumbled with his words. 'I – I – I didn't mean to say that. It was my first kiss and—'

'It was your first kiss?' Lucy looked a bit surprised. 'Blimey. You'd never have guessed.'

Was that a compliment?

'Well… yes,' said Jack. 'My first proper kiss. I did kiss Elizabeth Sladen on the cheek once but I suspect that doesn't count.'

Lucy raised an eyebrow, quizzically. 'Let me guess. She's a companion, right?'

'Yes. The best in my opinion. She played Sarah Jane Smith from—'

'Steady on there, Romeo. I'm the new girl in your life now, remember? Let's cut the talk of these other cute fantasy babes.'

Jack couldn't believe his ears.

Did this mean she wanted to go out with him?

'Er, right. Of course. Sorry.' He suddenly remembered that he still had his hand on her knee and he quickly jerked it back as if it had been burned.

Lucy grabbed his hand and put it back. 'No, that's OK, Jack. You're allowed to do that.'

Jack thought for a moment. He needed clarification of this whole situation.

Badly.

'So…does this mean we're kind of…an item now? As

in boyfriend and girlfriend? I mean, don't worry if we're not and you were just trying me out before you made a firm commitment. I wouldn't blame you. I mean, it's probably only right that you checked to see what you were getting before you agreed to that.'

'An item? Sure. Why not?'

Yes! Yes! Yes!

'So all this *Doctor Who* stuff really doesn't bother you, then?'

'Nope.'

Jack narrowed his eyes and stared at her more closely, checking for any signs of a twitching mouth ready to burst into a monumental, mocking grin before shouting, 'Of course I'm joking, you sad, freaky anorak boy!'

No – remarkably, she looked as if she meant what she was saying.

'I don't mind at all that you're into *Doctor Who*. This is just what you do at home – you've obviously got it totally in proportion and under control in your life.'

'What do you mean,' said Jack. This conversation was suddenly sounding like one of those Joey/Dawson moments from *Dawson's Creek* where everyone was a teenager but spoke really long sentences like adults.

'Well, you never mention it at school. I've known you for three months now and you've never uttered the words "Time And Relative Dimensions in Space" once.'

'True,' said Jack.

'You have other interests. You make me laugh and you are undoubtedly the cutest kid in our year. I'm the lucky one.'

Jack started to get some warm tingly feelings again. All over. Could it be true? Was she right that he was totally in control of this side of his life, and that he was otherwise a perfectly normal thirteen-year-old?

'Thank you.' Jack's face reddened now. 'I think you're really great too. I totally fancy you. I can't help it. I've thought of nobody else for months.'

From downstairs they heard a cry from Jack's mum. The food was ready.

Lucy stood up. 'Well, that's sorted then. Let's go out together, and have some fun. I might even be persuaded to watch an episode of *Doctor Who* with you.'

Jack's knees went wobbly, even though he was still sitting down. She really was the most perfect human being in the universe. Jack allowed himself to be pulled to his feet by Lucy. They were close together again. Jack leaned forward and gave Lucy a quick peck on the cheek. 'I think I'm going to be spending a lot less time in this bedroom from now on.'

'Not if I can help it, Casanova.' Lucy laughed.

Jack laughed too, and they left the room holding hands and headed downstairs for something to eat.

11
On Fire
for Thirteen

by Margaret Mahy

On Fire for Thirteen

Thirteen!

Thirteen!

There it was...coming towards her...ten days off...nine...eight... THIRTEEN!

The word made a sound in Emma's head, which seemed like a loud purring drumbeat followed by the note of a gong. Thirrr-TEEN!

Yet everyone turned thirteen. There was no way out of it. You couldn't say, 'Thirteen is an unlucky number. I'll stay on with twelve.' Or just jump straight through into fourteen.

Seven days...

Emma's friends, Adele, Laura, and Rachel were all thirteen and, though it mostly made no real difference, it sometimes seemed to Emma as if all the kids at school were climbing some huge tree, and her friends were clustered together springing and singing and having adventures on a bouncing bough just a little over her head. Boys like Griffy Watson and David Falconer seemed somehow sharper with Adele, Laura and Rachel, as if they were all exchanging secret messages a twelve-year-old could not read. When she was thirteen a new adventurous life might begin for her, and David Falconer might send secret messages in her direction.

'Just enjoy the last days of being twelve!' said Emma's mother, brushing down one of the twins. 'You'll never be twelve again in all your life.'

'Anyhow,' said Emma's big sister Judith, 'thirteen's just the same as being twelve except you get more homework. Big deal!'

Emma sighed. 'I sort of feel that when I'm thirteen life will be – I don't know – suddenly exciting.'

Judith laughed. 'Dream on!' she cried. 'It's just more school and Mum bossing you around. But hey – that Falconer kid down the road will suddenly be turned on by you!'

'Shut up!' yelled Emma, furious because there was a bit of truth in what Judith was saying.

'That's enough,' said their mother. But Emma was off and out, slamming the door after her.

Once outside she slid along the verandah that ran around three sides of the house and looked out across gardens, over the lawn and through the trees to the distant hills. Then, jumping skillfully over the wobbly top step (which Dad was always going to fix next Saturday or the Saturday after that) she raced towards the bottom of the garden. The first summer dryness was striking in and, even with the big water tanks to catch the run-off from their wide roof, they were going to have to be careful with water from now on. But early summer trees still bent fresh leaves towards her and, all alone at last, Emma danced, spinning herself, and singing as she spun.

'Twelve! Twelve!

Going, going, going!

Thirteen! Thirteen!

Growing, growing, growing!'

She was going to have a party. Laura, Adele and Rachel would come, of course, but other kids as well. The stereo would be pulled over by the sitting-room window so Emma and her friends could play CDs and rap around. It was going to be a really cool party…as long as it didn't rain.

Countdown! Six days…five…four…three…two…

The last day of being twelve.

'I'm going to a sleepover at Felicity's,' Judith said. 'But hey – I'll be back early in the morning to give you your present.' She gave Emma one of her rough bear hugs. 'Hang loose,' she cried and you could tell by the floppy way she ran out into the evening that she was hanging loose herself.

'The weather forecast is good,' said Emma's dad. 'I'll

do that step first thing tomorrow.'

'But clean out the fireplace now,' called her mother. 'I burnt a lot of rubbish this morning and it's full of ash.' The twins had just had their bath. They looked fresh and pink but they were both grizzling.

'Cot time for you two,' said Mum. She held out one arm to Rosie, and scooped Jasmine up in other. 'Bed for you heavy girls,' she sighed, beginning to climb the stairs.

'They're getting too big to carry,' Emma called after her.

'Don't worry! When you're thirteen you'll be able to hoist them up easily,' her mother called back over her shoulder.

Time for a read. Loving the quietness, Emma settled down in her favourite chair, looking for the right page.

But then door burst open. Emma's father staggered in, holding the elbow of his left arm with his right hand. His face, running with blood, was twisted up like a something out of a horror film. 'It's OK! It's OK!' he mumbled (though anyone could see it wasn't), 'I just…' (tumbling back into one of the good chairs, yelping as he did so.)

'Dad!' Emma screamed.

'I fell,' he said in that tight, almost mumbling

voice. 'That wobbly step…'

'Mum!' yelled Emma, just as her mother appeared at the top of the stairs, brushing her hands together. Looking down past Emma, she gave a cry.

'What's happened?'

'That wobbly step,' Emma's father repeated. 'I fell sideways and I…'

By now Mrs Kane was bending over him, while Emma hovered nearby, longing to help but not knowing how.

Her mother straightened. 'Emma,' she said, 'he'll be OK but I'm going to have to run Dad to the medical centre, so you'll have to baby-sit the twins for a couple of hours.'

'Of course Mum. Don't worry!' said Emma. She really wanted to drive over the hill with her parents but, even though the twins usually slept soundly, there was no way they could be left home alone. Her mother snatched up her car keys and then began guiding Emma's father around the verandah and down the side steps. Emma watched them cross the lawn and disappear into the trees by the garage.

She went back inside. The quietness which she had been enjoying a little earlier had turned ghostly…even threatening. She was never usually left alone for long. Mostly, when her parents went out together, the house was taken over by Judith, often with one or two friends, putting on CDs she was not usually allowed to play because they were too loud or because Mum hated the words.

So Emma read, while the silence deepened around her, until, at last, she decided she needed a cup of tea. But coming into the hall she stopped, horrified.

The very air around her had changed…looked smudgy…smelt smoky…

And no wonder!

Smoke was sliding out from under the closed kitchen door. Emma's heart hesitated, then thumped like a mad drum. Running to the kitchen door she opened it a crack, and immediately a great cloud of smoke rolled out at her. Through the smoke she glimpsed evil, bright spirits.

The kitchen was on fire.

Gasping and coughing, Emma slammed the door shut again. An urgent thought immediately elbowed into her. The twins! Their bedroom was directly above the burning kitchen.

Still coughing, Emma made for the stairs. Up! Up! On! On! Faster! Faster! Bursting into the twins' bedroom she was amazed to see that it was already hazy, smoke curling up through thin slits between the floorboards. Jasmine suddenly began coughing.

Desperately Emma hoisted her up and Jasmine began to wriggle too, complaining at being woken up so violently. One-handed, Emma let down the side of the other cot and scooped Rosie up with her other arm.

Jasmine screamed wildly, making Emma's head ring. Take a breath, Emma told herself. But not too deep a breath.

Then, half crouching under the rising wave of smoke Emma breathed carefully, hooked wriggling Rosie up over her left hip, and settled straining Jasmine against her right shoulder. Suddenly in charge, she thumped quickly but steadily down the stairs and into the hall, past the hall table where the phone squatted like a pale frog on the dark block of the phone directory.

Her father was a member of the Volunteer Fire Brigade. The beeper that summoned the volunteer firemen was always kept on the shelf above the table, but her father wasn't here and no one except Emma knew the house was on fire. The phone, Emma thought. Then... First things first! The twins!

The twins!

Somewhere off to her left Emma was aware of a smoldering glow, disappearing and then appearing again as she struggled with the front-door handle.

Suddenly something inside the house began screaming. For a dreadful moment she thought it might be Sam the cat and knew she must not even think about him. But it was the smoke alarm high on the wall behind her, finally waking up and crying out as if it were in pain.

Then Emma was outside, running around the verandah to the side steps. Down, down, carefully down…then over the lawn to the playhouse. Quickly she pushed first one twin and then the other inside the dark playhouse. She shut the door then twisted the loop of string around the hook, closing it.

'Thir-TEEN!' said the gong in her mind as if it were calling to her. 'I'm only twelve! This is too much responsibility too soon!' she shouted back at it as, turning, she looked at the house for the first time.

The verandah in front of the kitchen was now burning brightly, the flames reaching up the verandah posts, alive and eager. Through what had once been the kitchen window she could see the kitchen transformed to a dragon's cave of angry light. Smoke billowed out and up into the garden air.

She knew one of the fire brigade's rules was that she should run next door and ring them from there. But next door, for Emma, was a long way down the road. Instead she ran back to the side steps, along that part of the verandah which was not burning – not yet – and back into the hall, ringing with the urgent cries of the smoke alarm and thick with smoke. There was the hall table...there was the phone squatting on it. Taking a sideways breath of garden air and crouching low, Emma pushed in, felt for the phone, then pulled it towards the door.

The receiver trembled against Emma's ear and she realized that her hands were shaking. Be calm, she told herself. Take a breath. Take two! And a curious extra voice that was also her own said, Stretch ahead! Be thir-TEEN! Act responsibly!'

There it was...that gong again!

Still crouching, holding her finger as steady as she could, she dialled for emergency services. The phone rang its urgent note in her right ear cutting across the furious crying of the twins down in the playhouse.

A voice answered immediately. 'What service do you require?'

'Fire!' she said, almost screaming. 'The fire brigade!'

But another phone was already ringing.

'Fire service,' said another voice.

'Our house is on fire,' said Emma.

'Address,' said the voice.

'3 Kimberley Road, up from Barrington Bay...the

Marshall house…the road goes up from the Main road and…'

'Kimberley Road,' the voice said. 'I'm activating the call. Just hold on a moment there.'

Emma crouched lower, letting smoke sweep out over her.

'Now listen,' said the voice. 'Don't try to rescue anything…just get out of the house. If it's smoky get down on all fours and…'

'I'm out already. And I'm almost lying down,' said Emma.

'The fire brigade is on the way,' said the voice.

Somewhere from down by the gate someone was shouting. And from inside the house yet another shrill voice began giving a series of darting cries. The inside noise was her father's beeper calling from the shelf above the hall table. When that beeper sounded, automatically activated, her father usually raced for the car, so that he could drive to the fire station where his fireman's boots and coat and helmet would be waiting for him. But this time it was his house that was screaming in anguish, and he was far away in town at the doctor's. Remembering the looped serpent of hose beside the playhouse, Emma dropped the phone and made for the side steps.

The world rang with sound. In front of her in the

playhouse the twins yelled. Behind her the smoke alarm wailed, the fire roared and the beeper beeped...

'Hey!' a voice called, as someone came pounding across the lawn.

She recognized the voice...David Falconer.

'I was just coming down the hill and I saw the flames,' he yelled, running towards her.

By now Emma was uncoiling the hose, and turning on the tap. The hose leaped in her hands as if it were alive. Water shot out.

'Forget the hose. Just get the little kids out,' he ordered her in an impatient, panting voice.

'I already have,' Emma yelled sideways. 'Can't you hear them?'

'Ring the fire brigade,' David shouted, still running beside her as she headed back towards the house.

'I already have,' she cried back, and swung her hose towards the garden below the front verandah where the flames, finding new holds, were blazing wildly. The fire reared back, hissing...puffing up sudden new smoke. And now, another, distant voice began to sound...faintly at first...a wailing, warning voice, rising and falling, rising and falling...

The fire engine was on its way.

'Is there anything else we need to – to rescue?' said David uncertainly. A moment ago he had been ordering her around, but now he sounded as if he might do whatever she wanted done.

'We mustn't go inside,' said Emma. 'The place is full of smoke. The twins are safe, the cat can get out of a window I think, and the fire engine's coming. Listen!'

Already the siren was wailing more clearly. Emma imagined it racing closer and closer around the corners of the lower road.

'What can I do?' asked David Falconer, half putting out his hand to take the hose from her. Suddenly Emma found she was laughing. She felt David staring at her as if she had gone mad.

'Come to my birthday party tomorrow, why don't you,' she said. 'I'm turning thirteen.'

The verandah by the front steps was still blazing but it was not spreading before her swooping sword of water. The fire engine would almost be at the bottom of the hill by now.

'*Thir-TEE-a-EEE-a-EEE-a-EEEN*' the approaching fire engine seemed to be wailing. She had thought so much about turning thirteen that, even in the middle of such a terrible adventure, the word kept on pushing into her head.

'They'll need to connect to the water mains,' shouted David. 'Where are they? I'll show them.'

'We're not connected to the main water supply!' Emma yelled back. 'We've got water tanks. But they already know about our place. Dad's a volunteer fireman. And they'll be bringing a tanker with them anyway.'

Then (was it only a moment later?), there was even more noise in the world as the wailing engine swept up the drive and out onto the lawn. Men in helmets and boots began running towards the house.

And suddenly it was no longer her responsibility.

Emma was free to pass the hose over to one of the dark, helmeted figures…Mr Bain from the shop by the crossroads.

'Don't worry Emma,' he shouted. 'We're your team.'

Emma knew what he had shouted to her, but as the words reached her ears they twisted and she heard him say, 'Near thirteen!'

'Not until after midnight,' she shouted back, running for the playhouse, with David running beside her. As she reached the playhouse, and the crying twins, a hand grabbed her shoulder. Mum!

'What's happened?' her mother was shouting at her.

'Mum! I did the right things,' she shouted back. 'Mum! The twins. They're OK! They're OK!'

Although her mother sounded so terrified, Emma

had never been so pleased to see anyone – not even the fire brigade – in all her life. She rushed into her arms.

A whole twelve hours later, Emma woke up, smelling a wet burnt smell even before she was properly awake. Today was...today was...suddenly it all burst in on her. She had – she really had, at last, turned thirteen.

Her dressing gown lay on the end of the bed and as she put it on she heard the clock downstairs striking one...two...three. Emma imagined it striking thirteen in her honour but it stopped at nine. She ran out into the new day across wet carpet, with the burnt smell coming at her from every direction.

She could see skeletal beams through the blackened frame of the kitchen door. The hall table, the squatting phone and the grandfather clock were still in place, but were ringed in by boot tracks, garden dirt and strange twisting, muddy marks. Then she came out through the open front door...and there, sitting around the outside table, were her mother and father and Judith having a picnic breakfast. The twins were nearby too, playing in the playhouse they had hated so much the night before.

'Hi!' she called almost shyly. Faces turned towards her and then a huge, glad chorus of voices floated to meet her. 'Happy birthday!'

Her mother and Judith leaped up, running to hug her.

'Oh darling, we were lucky! So lucky!' her mother cried. 'So lucky to have you!'

She was laughing and crying a bit all at the same time.

'Well done, Sis,' said Judith, hugging her again.

Her father, his arm strapped up across his chest, came limping towards her.

'It was all my fault,' he said.

'It was nobody's fault,' her mother cried. 'It was just one of those things.'

'When Dad fell on that wobbly step he dropped ashes into the straw underneath the verandah,' Judith explained. 'And there must have been some live ashes somewhere in there…and they caught onto the straw under the kitchen and…'

'I usually check when I empty them out…' said her father.

'But hey – great way to turn thirteen,' said Judith.

'Actually I was still twelve when all that happened,' said Emma. 'It's funny isn't it? I mean, thinking that life would suddenly be adventurous when I turned thirteen, and then having all that stuff happen when I was still twelve. Twelve saying goodbye.'

'Well, your birthday cake has burned to a cinder,' said her mother. 'And the stove and the fridge are down, understandably.'

'I don't mind about not having a party,' said Emma. 'I'll have an extra big one when I'm eighteen and allowed to vote.'

But that afternoon something unexpected happened. Car after car pulled up outside their place and friends and neighbours came in with covered plates, sandwiches and cakes and little sausages, bowls of crisps, sweets and nuts. And presents! Books, hair ties, CDs of trendy bands.

'Oh thank you!' said Mum, over and over again. 'You're all so kind. There was no need, but we have got so much to celebrate.'

'Uh-oh!' whispered Judith leaning over to Emma. 'Look who's just arrived.'

There, coming in from the gate and across the scarred lawn, was David Falconer himself, holding a wrapped present under his arm.

'He's probably coming to see you,' said Emma, though she didn't really think so.

'No way! He told me you were just great,' said Judith. 'He's coming to check you out again, I can tell. You had that great adventure while you were still twelve, but here comes another...and this time you're

194

thirteen. Thirteen! Make the most of it. It'll only last a year.'

Emma looked towards David as he approached her and grinned.

12

You is a Man now, Boy

by Bali Rai

You is a Man now, Boy

My best mate, Will, had *his* thirteenth birthday party at the local church hall, across the road from the mosque. There was a mobile disco, provided by his 'uncle' Jake, and loads of our friends from school went along, the *girls* too. Will's mum, Sarah, got drunk and danced with everyone, ending up in the corner kissing his 'uncle'. And his gran made sandwiches with really nice fillings in them. I ate all the beef and horseradish ones that I could find and then stuffed myself even fuller with sausage rolls and mini-pizzas. I'd never had beef and horseradish before – I don't ever eat stuff like that at home – and I paid for it. I spent the most of next day on the loo. Will got loads of cool presents, but mainly the party was an excuse to drink the slightly 'funny' punch that his older sister, Jenna, made, and to act all grown-up. Will even got off with Olivia, one of our class mates, and the whole thing was really cool. I was so jealous.

See, my family, they're a bit old-fashioned. Well, OK, more than a bit. They're Punjabi and boy are they proud of it. My dad is always banging on about culture and pride and stuff. His idea of a birthday party doesn't involve getting an 'uncle' Jake to provide music or anything like that. I've never turned up at school with special handwritten invitations for everyone and I've never had a single party where I've asked the girls I know along. Or the boys for that matter.

Generally, the parties I've had involve my entire family getting together and eating tandoori chicken like a pride of lions would eat a pile of wildebeest, only with a bit less style. It's always the same, with the women in one room, listening to bhangra cassettes and drinking tropical fruit juice, and the men in another, with their lagers and their whisky and piles of food. Uncles grabbing me by the ear and telling me that I'm a 'good boy' and fat aunts hugging me to them until I nearly suffocate in the folds of their traditional Punjabi suits. There's always a big thing made of cutting the birthday cake, and then everyone takes their turn standing next to me, with whatever lame present they've given me, to have their photo taken. My mum's got a whole heap of nasty photos of me, wearing a shirt and tie, looking really embarrassed as some uncle and aunt show off the patterned sweater that they bought for me on their last trip to India.

And once the photography is over with I get to dance to really wack bhangra music from, *like*, twenty years ago, getting pulled around by cousins and aunts and great uncles and the like. I mean how *cool* is that, man? Yeah, not very. After that the men go off down the pub and I get left with all the other kids, most of them looking a bit sick 'cos they've stuffed ten slices of the birthday cake into their gobs and washed them down with the Asda cola that my dad insists on buying by the truck load. 'Bloody same thing innit?' he'll often say at the top of his voice when we're out shopping and I ask him to buy proper Coke.

So I've never invited even Will along to one of my parties because of the 'die at school on Monday morning from mega-shame' factor. Just imagine what the girls I know would say? After my twelfth birthday, Olivia asked me what I had done, and I just shrugged and blagged that I'd gone down to see my favourite cousin in London, and that we'd gone on that big spinning wheel thing before loafing around the shops and that. She seemed impressed but she can't have been *that* bothered 'cos she snogged Will at his thirteenth party even though me and Will had an agreement that she'd be my girlfriend first. I don't get girls, but then I don't get my latest X-Box game either and there's instructions with that.

A couple of weeks ago it was my thirteenth, on a Saturday. I told my parents the week before that I didn't want another family party. I talked up all this stuff about not being a kid anymore, being a teenager and that. At first my dad, who resembles an Indian version of Homer Simpson, looked a bit worried. But then my older brothers, Jit and Satnam, took my side and said that I was a man now.

'We'll take you down the pub, innit Jag – get you a real drink and that,' Satnam told me.

I didn't want him to think that I was a kid so I nodded and said the pub would be great. But that's not what I wanted to say. I wanted to say that I was hoping for a more grown-up party, like Will's, held at the local church hall, with all my friends from school invited. But I knew that it wouldn't happen. It was about as likely as my dad eating beef and horseradish sandwiches. I didn't think the pub, grown-up as it was, was really my idea of fun – not that I knew, I'd never been in one. I was thinking that an afternoon at the cinema, maybe Pizza Hut, might be possible. Like Simran Sangha's parents let her do. I mean they were Punjabi so surely that would be all right. Oh no – not for my dad.

'No pub – too young. And Pizza eat at bloody home, boy. Ju mays well be setting fire to money, idiot. And ju watching all films on DBD playing anyways so what ju need go cinema for?'

'But dad…'

'Leave it, Jagtar – we having nice party at home – just family.'

And he left it at that as I sulked in my seat and a fit Bollywood actress danced around on the TV screen, with my mum glued to her every move.

On the actual day of my birthday I was in the park watching my brothers playing football for a local team for most of the afternoon. My dad had relented about the family party and instead my mum had made a load of food which we were going to have in the evening – chicken, lamb, samosas, fish pakora, that kind of stuff. It was going to be a quiet night, just the immediate family, and maybe a couple of uncles with their families. Not what I wanted, but then it wasn't going to be the torture that it might have been either.

The match was OK in the end and my brothers' team, Guru Gobind Khalsa FC, won three-nil. There were only like five fights on the pitch and only two off it. My brothers have been trying to get me to play for the youth team but I'm sticking to the school team, where things are more like the matches you see on TV. Safe.

After the game my brothers stood around with

their team, drinking from cans of Coke and swearing at the other team in Punjabi. Every single player then changed into various versions of the Man Utd shirt, and most of them made their way across the park, over the road and into the pub. Jit and Satnam hung back with a couple of our cousins, Guvvy and Tej, and talked about football.

'We're gonna batter Aston Villa, man,' said Tej, talking about the Man Utd game that was into its second half.

'Easy – may as well give us the points, innit,' replied my brother, Jit, before taking a long drink from his can of Coke.

'I reckon Nistelrooy will score first,' added Satnam.

'Scholesy more like…man is *bad*,' argued Guvvy, flicking his fingers together for effect.

'How 'bout you, birthday boy – who your bunch of no-hopers got today then?' asked Satnam.

It took a few seconds before it dawned that my brother was talking to me. I looked up at him and shrugged. 'Middlesborough, I think,' I told him.

I knew it was Middlesborough but I was keeping quiet about my team because we were doing so badly.

'Bloody *Liverpool Schmiverpool* – you wanna get yerself a proper team, you girl,' laughed Tej.

'But you used to be a Liverpool fan,' I told him.

'I seen the light tho', bro – like in them Bollywood films, innit. *Ganesh baba-ji* shone him light down pon my life and shown me the way...' he replied, as I wondered what the hell he was talking about.

'Now what we gonna do for your birthday then?' asked Satnam.

'We're having a party at home ain't we?' I said.

'Yeah – but that's later,' added Jit. 'What we gonna do now, innit?'

I wondered what they were on about. I didn't actually want to do anything with them. I had been hoping to go round to Will's house.

'How old you gonna be?' asked Guvvy.

'Thirteen,' I told him.

'Well then you is a man now, boy,' laughed Tej. 'Only one thing for it...'

'Take you down the pub like my old man did when I was that age,' agreed Guvvy.

My brothers grinned at me.

'It's an old Punjabi custom, Jag. You got to *drink* like a man before you can *think* like a man,' said Jit.

Everyone gave him a funny look except for me. I was too worried.

'Actually I don't wanna go to the—' I began.

'No brother of mine's gonna chicken out of the

pub,' said Satnam, sternly.

'But *Dad* drinks in there,' I replied quickly, trying to get out of it.

'He ain't gonna be in there *now*, is he,' reassured Jit.

'Come then you girls – what we waitin' for,' laughed Tej, grabbing me in a bear hug.

I found myself being carried along by my cousin, who was big and fat and smelly. I was kicking my legs out but he had me in a firm hold and only put me down when we reached the main road.

'But I'm underage,' I protested.

'There's ways round that, you *phoodah*,' laughed Guvvy, swearing at me in Punjabi.

'But…' I began, as we ran across the main road in front of speeding cars.

I wondered if Will had ever been to the pub and decided that he probably hadn't. And then, suddenly, going to the pub seemed like a good idea. I thought about how I would tell my friends about it the following Monday. Acting all grown-up and that. *Yeah, man – I was like, you know, down the pub wiv my brothers.* That'll impress Olivia, I thought to myself as we walked round to the back of the pub and out into the beer garden. The rest of the footballers were there, milling around, holding drinks, and there were loads of other people too. I started to feel a bit self-conscious, wondering if they were all looking at me because I was underage. Satnam led us to the very back of the garden, by a wooden gateway that led into an alley at the back, and as we approached a wooden picnic bench the two girls who were there before us got up to leave.

'Don't go on our account, ladies,' said Jit, all cheesily, like he was presenting a game show or something.

The girls looked at him and then at each other, screwed up their faces in disgust and left.

'What you drinkin' then lads?' asked Guvvy, reaching for his wallet.

Almost immediately the rest of them started to say that they'd get the drinks. It was a ritual that my family went through whenever money was involved. Often an aunt would give me a tenner for my birthday and my mum would refuse it, and they'd pass the money to and fro for about five minutes before I got to keep it anyway. Or my dad would want to buy food on a family trip to somewhere like Alton Towers, only for one of my uncles to say that no, he'd get the food, and then another to say it, and another. Eventually my dad would get the food anyway. The same thing happened at the pub.

'Nah, nah – I'll get 'em,' replied Guvvy, after a five minute discussion.

'Well in that case I'll have a Pils,' Satnam told him.

'Bacardi an' Coke,' said Jit and Tej together.

'Wha' 'bout you, bro ?' asked Guvvy, looking at me.

'Coke,' I told him.

'Better put a likkle bit of Bacardi in there too,' said Satnam.

'Nah – I'm OK,' I replied.

For some reason I had butterflies in my stomach. I was feeling really nervous.

'Bacardi for the birthday boy,' said Jit.

Guvvy turned to go to the bar.

'Make it a small one, though,' Satnam demanded.

'No worries,' replied Guvvy, grinning.

We sat and chatted nonsense until Guvvy returned with the drinks. He put mine in front of me as he sat down and grinned at me, but I didn't pick it up. I just sat there for a while, looking at it, as the butterflies increased.

'What you waitin' for then? Have your drink, little brother,' urged Jit, winking as he spoke.

'In a minute,' I replied.

I looked around at the other customers but none

of them seemed interested in my presence. I picked up my drink and sniffed at it.

'What – is you a dog or somethin'?' laughed Satnam. 'Just drink it, man – it ain't nuttin'.'

'But I've never had an alcoholic drink before,' I protested.

'It ain't gonna hurt, man,' laughed Tej.

'*Thirteen* today – act like a man,' added Jit.

I looked at it again and then put the glass to my lips, taking the smallest sip. It tasted like Coke only there was a serious tang to it – it was bitter.

'Urgh!'

'Shut up and drink it,' said Satnam, shaking his head at me.

I stuck two fingers up at him and looked around again. Satisfied that I wasn't being watched I drank a little more, screwing up my face at the taste. I drank some more and found that the initial bitterness had gone. It tasted kind of sweet now, sugary like flat cola, although it burned my throat. I put the glass down and looked around for the third time. No one was watching me at all. Over by the entrance to the garden I spotted a couple of lads from school, Year Tens, with their football crowd. One of them had what looked like a lemonade in his hands and the other one, a bottle of orange juice. I thought about how impressed Olivia would be if she could see me, acting all grown-up and that. I picked up my drink and had some more.

By the time that I had relaxed a bit, the glass was half-empty. I didn't feel any different, not like I had expected to. I didn't feel anything at all really. Just kind of warm inside, as the sun shone down on the beer garden and I listened to my family talk about girls and football and stuff. The lads from my school had moved closer to us and I caught their attention. They both nodded at me and then looked at each other. I got up and walked over, my head feeling a bit light. I took my drink with me.

'Yes, man,' I said loudly, as I approached them.

'Easy Jag,' replied Parmy, the taller of the two.

'What you doin' in here?' asked the shorter one.

'Havin' a drink with my brothers, Gary,' I boasted, trying to act as cool as I could manage.

'What's that – Coke?' asked Parmy.

'Nah man – it's my birthday so I'm having a *real* drink.'

'Get off it man!' replied Gary. 'Like they'd get you a *real* drink. You're only in year seven or somethin'.'

'*Serious,*' I said, suddenly feeling all brave. 'Try it if you don't believe me.'

I offered Gary the glass and he took a sip.

'*Raas!* That's definitely Bacardi, Parm – the kid ain't blaggin'.

Gary handed the glass to Parmy who took a sip too.

'Tastes a bit strong though,' said Parmy.

We stood and chatted as my head grew a bit lighter. I was totally cool now, feeling all grown up, chillin' with two older lads from school. Maybe they'd talk to me at school a bit more now, I thought. I could even hang around with them. It would beat talking about computer games with the geeks who were my age. I was just about to say aloud what I was thinking when my brother, Jit, walked up.

'What you havin' bro?' he asked.

I shrugged like it didn't bother me in the slightest. 'Nuther one, man,' I replied.

'Yes – bad bwoi!' laughed Gary. 'Better watch it though – them Bacardis's gonna lick out yer head man!'

'Ain't nuttin',' I told him, like I was some serious, big-time drinker.

Gary and Parmy grinned at each other. They were

smirking. I didn't think that I'd shouted but Parmy gave me a nudge and grinned some more. 'Keep it down, kid – the whole pub heard that.'

'Don't care,' I said, turning to head back to my seat.

'Mind yuh motion!' laughed Gary as I weaved through the crowd.

I was feeling more and more woozy by then and I'm sure I stepped on a couple of toes as I passed. By the time that I reached the bench where my family were, I had to sit down. My mouth was really dry and I had this strange feeling in my stomach, like it was being frozen from the inside out. Satnam asked me if I was OK and for a moment I just looked at him.

'Cool, man,' I replied at last, looking away.

When Jit returned with my second drink about fifteen minutes later, I sat and looked at it for what seemed to me like ages. I could feel beads of sweat forming just where my hair met my forehead, and the frozen belly feeling was turning into a need to belch. I swallowed a load of air and then some more, trying desperately to keep a straight face so that my brothers wouldn't think that there was anything wrong with me. Only there was.

My head was spinning and I was finding it really difficult to keep my eyes open. I could hear my brothers talking but my brain didn't seem to be turning their words into anything that was making sense. All around me everyone was busy socialising, and I started to get all paranoid, thinking that people were pointing at me, and talking about me.

I looked down at my drink, desperate to belch so that the wind trapped in my belly could find somewhere to go. I picked up my drink and took a sip. A wave of nausea swept over me and I had to swallow really hard so that I didn't throw up. I looked at my brothers, both of them laughing and joking, and not really paying me any attention. Another wave of nausea hit, and my stomach churned over and over. I put the drink down and stood up suddenly.

'Goin' the loo,' I mumbled, not waiting for my brothers to reply.

I weaved my way through the crowd, trying not to look anyone in the eye, just in case they realised that I was off it. The toilets were back near the entrance to the beer garden, by the door to the bar, and I could see them getting closer and closer. But the rushes of sickness were taking over by then and twice I had to put my hand to my mouth as I nearly threw up. I edged past Gary and Parmy, who I'm sure were laughing at me, and headed quickly for the toilet door. My stomach seemed to clench tight and the sweat on my forehead began to freeze. Just a bit further, I thought to myself.

I didn't make it. As I reached the door, someone stepped out of it. My head reared back of its own accord and the contents of my stomach arced through the air, all over the man in front of me. I felt myself collapse. As I looked up at the blue sky and white wisps of cloud, I heard a familiar voice.

'*Jagtar?*'

And then my dad leant over me, covered in my puke, looking like he wanted to kill me. I tried to smile but my eyes closed over and I was out for the count.

It turned out that my cousin Guvvy had spiked my first drink from a flask of home-made brew that he had with him. It's called 'desi' in Punjabi, and it's really strong. My dad, after he'd got me home, and changed his clothes, seemed to calm down about it all. I dunno what happened in the five hours that I was out for the count, but when I woke up, hot and sweaty in my bed, he was standing over me, smiling.

'Have you become a man today then?' he asked jokingly, in Punjabi.

I groaned and a shooting pain bolted through my

head. I blinked at him before I spoke.

'If that's bein' a man,' I said in a croak, 'then I don't wanna be one.'

My dad was *still* laughing five minutes later.

13

Space–Alien Mothers and the Non–Wild, Wild Child

by Karen McCombie

Space-Aliens Mothers and the Non-Wild, Wild Child

The first time I saw my dad on telly, I screamed.

But then I was only three, and he was playing the part of a giant, extra-terrestrial lizard from the planet Tharg.

'It's me under the costume and make-up, Joey babes!' he had to tell me three thousand times before I calmed down.

But it taught me a valuable lesson – things aren't always what they seem. Scaley/scary lizards can be lovely dads underneath. Your best mate's smiling, friendly-looking mother could be an evil space alien in disguise.

Oh, yes.

Charlie's always been kind of funny about having me back to hers, and now that I'm finally here I understand why. I mean, it can't be easy having an evil space alien for a mother, can it?

I've only just discovered this shocking fact in the last ten minutes or so. Actually, I can hardly believe that just quarter of an hour ago I was happily strolling along the street with Charlie, heading towards her house, sharing a packet of Minstrels and having a conversation about why pigeons are so fat when they don't seem to eat anything except road grit. And now…well, now I seem to have entered a parallel universe.

How careless of me.

'So, Joanna, what do you call *that*?'

I'm sitting in the kitchen of 'The Willows', 19 Turnham Road, which probably *seems* ordinary (in a swanky way) if you're gawping at it from the pavement. On the other side of the perfectly polished table is Charlie's supposedly ordinary mum, who is pointing in the general direction of my face while she talks. In answer to her question I'm tempted to say, 'Uh, I call it my nose, Mrs Thomson. At least, we call them "noses" on Earth. What do they call them on your planet?'

Course, I don't say that, because I am a nice(ish), polite(ish) human, and even when faced with evil space aliens and their sarky digs, I remember my manners. So instead of blasting Charlie's mum with an equally sarky comeback, I just blink at her instead and self-consciously touch my nose.

'No, no!' Mrs Thomson laughs at me, in that way people do when they're trying to helpfully let you know that you're an idiot. 'I meant your eyes, Joanna!'

That doesn't really help. What's she on about? What

do I call my eyes?! I dunno…Bob? Eddie? I feel a blush of confusion flush over my face, as my fried brain struggles to come up with an answer to this bizarre question. I had the same problem knowing how to respond to: 'Is it *difficult* for your mother to afford proper school uniform?' (as she stared a hole through my denim shirt) or: 'Purple? How odd!' (as she checked out my painted, bitten nails). It's just really confusing when the words sound horrible but the mouth that's saying them is fixed in a grin…

I glance over at Charlie for help, hoping she can interpret what her evil space alien mother is trying to say, but my best friend appears to be fascinated by the contents of her fridge. (If she stands there much longer, she'll end up with frost on her fringe.)

'That stuff around your eyes, I mean!' Mrs Thomson laughs again in that bright, breezily patronising way of hers. 'Is your mother happy to let you wear that?'

From the tone of her voice, it would be easy to suspect I'd smeared glitter or tar or *jam* or something over the top half of my face, instead of just running a little bit of black eyeliner inside the lower lids.

But maybe Mrs Thomson has a reason for over-reacting; maybe wearing eyeliner is a serious criminal offence here on the planet Sponggg, or wherever it is I landed when I stepped through Charlie's front door, or portal, and veered into this parallel universe...

Let me back up a bit here. My world works like this:

1) Joanna's on my birth certificate, but everyone calls me Joey.
2) I live with my mum in a nice council flat on an OK estate.
3) My parents are what's called 'amicably' divorced (i.e. they don't loathe each other).
4) I speak to my dad all the time, although I won't be seeing so much of him now he's got this new job up North.
5) At school, I do all right in most subjects; I'm quite liked by most of the teachers (OK, so the deputy head doesn't exactly *love* my take on school uniform), and I get on with most people (though some of the boys have started calling me 'Morticia' 'cause of the eyeliner thing).
6) My best mate (as of the last four months) is Charlie Thomson.

The thing is, in this parallel universe, all of that's still true, only in a weird, skewed way – thanks to Charlie's evil space alien mother.

Not that Mrs Thomson looks like one; oh no. But aliens are cunning that way, aren't they? They disguise themselves as humans so no one flips out at the sight of their mutant lobster claws and eyes on wobbly stalks. I mean, when Charlie first introduced me a long quarter of an hour ago, all I saw was a blonde, smiley woman, glancing up from some fancy homes magazine she was flicking through. Then as soon as the first hellos, pleased to meet yous were out of the way, she started slipping up. The corners of her mouth were still pointing reassuringly upwards, but the questions and comments she directed my way started stinging like I was starkers in a nettle patch ('You're in the top stream at school, same as Charlotte? *How* surprising!').

As she looked me up and down, the manicured nails she was tap-tapping on the table almost began turning into mutant lobster claws in front of my very eyes. And *that's* when it dawned on me that Charlie's mum *had* to be an evil space alien. Or maybe she was just plain evil. Either way, I suddenly began to feel horribly sorry for Charlie...

'Joey's mum says she doesn't mind Joey experimenting with clothes and make-up,' Charlie suddenly announces, angrily thunking two glasses and a carton of orange juice down on the table, so that some of it splooshes out. 'She says she did it herself when she was a teenager.'

'Well, it seems to me,' shrugs Mrs Thomson, reaching over for some kitchen roll to mop up the spill, 'if you've made mistakes in the past yourself, it's a bit cruel to just sit back and watch others make a fool of themselves too, don't you think?'

Charlie's mum is directing her words at her daughter, but it's plain as the nose on my human face that the barb is aimed at 'foolish' little me and my 'irresponsible' mum.

And that's the problem: in Mrs Thomson's world, through her eyes (on the ends of their wobbly alien stalks), I am someone I hardly recognise. To her...

1) My name is Joanna, not some silly, tomboy-ish nickname.

2) I live with my single-parent mother in a trashy flat on a run-down, crime-filled estate.

3) My parents are divorced (the shock, the horror, the shame!).

4) I probably never see my no-good father (if I even know who he is).

5) Me wearing purple nail varnish + eyeliner = delinquent who spends most of her afternoons in detention.

6) I am a bad influence on 'Charlotte' and will lead her astray.

'Which way's the loo?' I ask, suddenly desperate to get away from the interrogation and the sarcasm for a few short, blissful minutes. And while I'm pretending to pee I can try to figure out how exactly I can escape from this place without seeming too rude (not that Mrs Thomson is exactly holding back in the rudeness department).

'It's in front of you at the top of the stairs,' says Charlie, her face white and pinched, her eyes staring into mine and flashing 'sorry, sorry, sorry!' at me.

I hadn't realised that Charlie's evil space alien mother had zapped my body with some paralyzing mind-ray, but as soon as I take my first step into the hallway I must be out of her psychic range. Every tense muscle begins to relax. By the time I've hurried up the stairs and closed the bathroom door behind me, I'm so relieved I practically slither down onto the cool, grey-slate floor.

'Wow...' I mumble, taking in the old-fashioned, claw-footed bath standing in the middle of a room that's bigger than my living room. Mum would absolutely *love* this – not just the stadium-sized bathroom, I mean, but the whole place. Much as she's made our flat kind of cosy, this is her dream house, the sort of house single social workers (i.e. Mum) and mostly out-of-work actors (i.e. Dad) could never afford in a million years of social working and doing occasional voiceovers for discount carpet warehouses.

Y'know, it's funny how – all the times she's been round to mine – Charlie's always gone on about how great our flat is. She's never seemed to notice that the carpet is second-hand and hideous, or that the throws on the sofa are covering a lot of floral horribleness that's been scratched to shreds by some former owner's cat. She's eaten her tea off brightly coloured plates that don't match and drunk out of mugs that *only* match 'cause there's a chip out of every one of them. She's sat on our one, wobbly-legged stool while my mum's braided her blonde hair. She's learned the right way to use the handle on the loo so that it doesn't fall off. And all the time, she must have been thinking how crummy-by-comparison my house is to hers.

Or maybe she doesn't think that at all, I muse, clambering up on to my feet and turning on the chunky cold water tap in the sink. I can't see Charlie's evil space alien mother braiding her hair with those mutant lobster claws of hers...

The splash of cool water on my face chills my head as well as my skin. And here's what instantly flips into my mind now it's clearer...in the few months that we've been best mates, Charlie has never said anything bad about her parents, but mainly because she's hardly said anything about them at all. Every time I've asked her a question about them, she's shrugged it off. So best mates or not, the only things I knew about her home life, up till now, was that a) she lived with both her parents, and b) she lived with them in a house in one of those streets where the families drive their kids to school in Range Rovers and Land Cruisers and other cars that are practically as big as my flat.

So I guess, deep down, I've been kind of worried that Charlie hadn't invited me round here before 'cause of her living where she lives and me coming from where I come from. I thought she was embarrassed about me. Now I'm starting to suspect that she's embarrassed all right – but about her own mum...

'You've got to develop a rhinoceros skin,' I tell my reflection, as I run a finger underneath my eyes to tidy the smears of black eyeliner.

The rhinoceros thing; that's what Dad told me once, about all the auditions he's been up for over the years. But what am I auditioning for? Being Charlie's friend? I thought I already was, at least as far as Charlie was concerned.

But it's time to test out the new rhinoceros skin

against the mind-rays – I can't hide out here any more, or Mrs Thomson will probably suspect me of nicking her dental floss…

'Well, I just don't see what the attraction is,' I hear a certain smug, self-righteous voice say, as I come out of the bathroom and hesitate – breath held – on the first floor landing.

'Look, Mum – Joey's just really nice, OK?' comes Charlie's sharp-edged reply.

Er…that'll be me they're talking about, then.

I hear a sort of snorting sound, the type that's an infuriating short cut to saying, 'Yeah, like I'm going to believe that!'. I have one foot hovering on the first step of the stair, but don't have the bottle to take it; forget rhinoceros – my skin feels thin as a newborn kitten's.

'Charlotte, the bottom line is that I don't want you hanging out with some…some wild child! I don't see why you can't spend more time with Rhea Martin. When we were round at her parents' on Saturday, they said they hardly see you any more!'

Eek…! *Me*, a *wild* child?! Just 'cause I wear a denim shirt instead of a school blouse and dark nail varnish I got free off the cover of *Bliss*?! And I'm sorry, but if Mrs Thomson thinks Rhea Martin is better company for her daughter than me, well, that's like saying Charlie would be better off playing chicken in rush-hour traffic than sitting at home in front of *Blue Peter*.

Does she have any idea what Rhea Martin is actually *like?* (Answer: no, obviously not.)

I feel dizzy, and realise I'm still holding my breath. 'Count to ten as you breathe in slowly, and ten to let it all out. Really calms stage fright,' I remember Dad once telling me, when he'd caught me hyperventilating over an upcoming chemistry test.

As I begin counting, I hold tight to the banister rail and I think of Rhea Martin. Rhea 'butter-wouldn't-melt-in-her-mouth' Martin, known to teachers as a bright girl, from a respectable family; known to everyone in our year as a bully, and trouble with a capital T, R, O, U, B, L *and* E.

It was because of Rhea Martin that I ended up being best mates with Charlie, or more particularly, why Charlie became best mates with me. If I hadn't walked into the girls' loos at the school party when I did, Rhea would have landed her so-called friend Charlie in one whole heap of hassle. Knowing them both just a little bit, I'd nodded hello when I came out of a cubicle and saw Rhea smoking and Charlie looking fed up. Half a second later, as I washed my hands, I saw two things: in the mirror – Miss McCarthy, our deputy head, strolling in; out of the corner of my eye, Rhea Martin hurriedly shoving her cigarette into Charlie's hand.

'Chuck it!' I hissed above the rush of cold water to a confused-looking Charlie, the only one in the room whose teacher radar hadn't gone off.

I still don't know why Charlie decided to take notice of nobody old me, but she did – and tossing that cigarette out of the open window onto the grass below not only saved her from being suspended, it ended one friendship (with Rhea) and started a brand new one (with me).

'I just don't have much in common with Rhea any more, all right?' I hear Charlie say now.

'Oh, don't be ridiculous! Give me one good reason you two aren't friends these days!'

Uh-oh – Charlie can't exactly come clean about Rhea, can she? Not without owning up to all the trouble she'd nearly got into herself, all because she had the misfortune of being Rhea Martin's official best mate...

Taking a deep, calming breath and willing my skin to thicken, I start stomping loudly down the stairs.

'Ah, there you are, Joanna!' smirked Mrs Thomson. 'We were just about to send out a search party!'

I don't care about the sarcasm right now; I'm just glad that she's dropped the subject of Rhea Martin. And you can bet that Charlie is too.

'Your orange juice,' Charlie murmurs, smiling a secret thank-you smile at me.

'Well, sit down, Joanna – no point making the room look untidy! Ha!'

I guess I'm stuck here till I finish my drink. Wonder how many gulps it'll take to get through it?

'So…' Mrs Thomson starts up, tap-tapping her nails on the table again. 'Tell me more about your family, Joanna. Your mum; does she work?'

Charlie seems to know as well as I do that in evil space alien that translates as 'Does she live off benefits?'.

'Joey's mum's a child protection officer for the social services department,' Charlie butts in before I can answer.

'Oh!' says Mrs Thomson, the smugness and the smile fading from her face. 'And, um, what about your father?'

'He's in Manchester,' I tell her, wondering what her tiny alien mind will make of that. 'He's just got a part in a new police drama thing Channel 4 are doing up there.'

Charlie's mum looks about as surprised as if she's just had her bottom pinched by Homer Simpson. I'm not sure what this means – my powers of alien translation have failed.

But I get it as soon as she says the name of the programme (which she loves) and susses out who my dad is (she loves him too). And now I see myself reflected back in her human-looking eyes and realise she's not scowling at a wild child anymore; she's gazing in amazement at the daughter of someone off the telly. How pathetic.

'Listen, I know this is ridiculous, Joanna,' Mrs Thomson suddenly giggles, as Charlie stands behind her frowning in horror, 'but you couldn't get your dad's autograph for me, could you?'

Charlie is now standing right behind her mum's chair, pretending to strangle her. I have to take a gulp of orange juice just to hide the massive grin on my face.

'Actually, I've just had a thought, Joanna – as you and Charlotte are such good friends, maybe next time your dad is here in London, your family could come round for dinner!'

When the orange juice snorts out of my nose, I guess Mrs Thomson thinks it's 'cause I'm choking – which I am, but only because laughing and swallowing is a very, very bad combination.

'Are you OK?' Charlie asks, with a knowing twinkle in her eye.

'Yeah, fine,' I cough a bit in reply, now hiding my

grin behind the piece of kitchen roll she's handed me. 'But I think I'd better be going home.'

Charlie and her mum both come to the front door to wave me off; Charlie with her pale hand and Mrs Thomson with her mutant lobster claw.

'See you at school tomorrow, Joey!' Charlie calls out.

'Yeah, see you!' I call back, glad to be out in the real world again.

The real world where pigeons get fat on road grit, where wearing purple nail varnish isn't a crime, where mums are ordinary and not evil space aliens (or even silly, shallow snobs, which is just as bad).

And best of all, where I'm Joey – proud to be a non-wild, wild child...

Turn over to read more

about the authors...

Paul Bailey is a writer and broadcaster of great renown. Two of his novels for adults, *Peter Smart's Confessions* and *Gabriel's Lament* have been shortlisted for the Booker Prize For Fiction. This is his first story for younger readers.

Kevin Brooks won the 2003 Branford Boase Award for a best first novel with *Martyn Pig*. It was also shortlisted for the Carnegie Medal. His subsequent novels, *Lucas, Kissing the Rain* and *Candy* have all been published to much critical acclaim.

Eoin Colfer's series of bestselling novels featuring Artemis Fowl have made him an international children's literary megastar. His signing sessions are sell-outs and his sense of humour is legendary.

Mary Hooper has been writing children's books for over twenty years and has written for readers of all ages with great success. Her teenage novel, *Megan*, won the North East Book Award in 2001.

Margaret Mahy is New Zealand's most prolific and best-loved children's author. Throughout her career she has won many awards including the Carnegie Medal,

The Boston Globe – Horn Book Award, The Esther Glen Award and the New Zealand Post Children's Book Award.

Karen McCombie began her writing career working on magazines such as *J17* and *Sugar*. Her *Ally's World* series of novels, which have been translated in many countries, have made her a household name among young teenagers.

John McLay is a literary scout for children's books and a reviewer. His contribution to this anthology is his first piece of published fiction. His business card, designed by illustrator Nick Sharratt, is one of his most prized possessions.

Helen Oyeyemi's first novel for adults, *The Icarus Girl*, was published in January 2005. It was written while she was still at school, studying for her A Level exams.

Bali Rai is an accomplished author of books for teenage readers and is a winner of the Leicester Book Award and The Angus Book Award. His first novel, *(un)arranged Marriage*, was shortlisted for the Branford Boase Award in 2002.

Marcus Sedgwick won the Branford Boase Award with his first novel, *Floodland*. He was then shortlisted for the *Guardian* Children's Book Award, the Blue Peter Award and the Carnegie Medal for *The Dark Horse*.

Eleanor Updale studied history at St. Anne's College, Oxford, before becoming a producer of TV and radio current affairs programmes for the BBC. Her first children's novel, *Montmorency*, won the Silver Smarties Prize and the Medway Book Award, and has been shortlisted for the Blue Peter Book Award and the Branford Boase Award.

Jean Ure had her first book published when she was sixteen and is the bestselling author of over a hundred books for children and teenagers. As well as writing light-hearted, humorous novels (recently praised by The *Guardian* as 'inventive and funny'), she has a long and distinguished record of tackling sombre themes in a positive way.

Kay Woodward has written many bestselling books, including *Robot Wars: The Ultimate Guide* and *The Big Jungle Hunt*. For many years she was a children's book editor but she is now an established author of fiction.